The Secret's in the Folding

Published by
Pewter Rose Press
17 Mellors Rd,
West Bridgford
Nottingham, NG2 6EY
United Kingdom
www.pewter-rose-press.com

First published in Great Britain 2010

ISBN 978-0-9560053-6-6

British Library Cataloguing in Publication Data
A catalogue record for this book is available from the British
Library

Cover design by www.thedesigndepot.co.uk

Printed and bound in Great Britain

Pewter Rose Press
www.pewter-rose-press.com

CONTENTS

ACKNOWLEDGEMENTS

I am grateful to several competition judges and organisers for their encouragement: The Scotland on Sunday/ Macallan Awards, Neville Moir and team at Polygon Birlinn, Janice Galloway, Michel Faber, James Roberston, Suhayl Saadhi, Ron Butlin, Sarah Jacob (Woman's Own), Helena Nelson and team at Happenstance Press, the team behind the Neil Gunn Competition, Jan Fortune-Wood (Cinnamon Press), The Soutar Prize administrators (Perth & Kinross Council), Duncton Cottage Animal Sanctuary Competition.

Many of these stories had a first airing in print or on radio, thanks to these brave editors: Kirsty Williams at BBC Radio Scotland, Julian Stuart formerly of The Guardian Weekly, John Hudson and Chrys Salt (Markings magazine), Magi Gibson, (Ironstone magazine), James Scott (InkerMen Press) and Mslexia magazine.

My appreciation to the Mayor and staff of Bydgoszcz International Book Festival for generous hospitality, readings and publication in Polish. Thanks to Thiago Tizzot of *Arte e Letra* journal, Curitiba for translation and publication in Brazilian Portuguese and the warm welcome given to a gringo writer. For encouragement, and the fantastic food, coffee and literary ambience of Café Quintana, Curitiba, thanks to Rogério Pereira of *Rascunho* journal.

I owe a great deal to Ajay Close and her reflections, guidance and passion for literature, to Merryn Glover and to the Soutar House Writers for support, reading and thoughtful critique.

The Captain's Woman owes more than she admits to the real life stories of Lampião and Maria Bonita, while President Medici's lover is pure invention.

This collection would not have seen the light of day without the insight and wise editing of Anne McDonnell at Pewter Rose Press.

Lastly, I am indebted to Athayde Tonhasca and the Thackeray family: Sheila, Sheila and Bill for unflagging support, enthusiasm for reading my stories and for having the courage to mention the bad as well as the good. Athayde has contributed more than he knows as an inspiring companion in my explorations of Brazil, its culture and history.

FOREWORD

Prepare yourself for a journey.

All but one of the stories in this collection are set in Brazil (the exception, set in Edinburgh, features Brazilian migrant workers). In the following pages you'll find slum dwellers, girl soldiers, maids, Carnaval dancers, competitive cake-bakers, beauticians, emancipated slaves, sugar cane cutters, hospital janitors, and even a mermaid. You'll travel from cosmopolitan Rio to the rural backwater of Bom Jesus, from the remote upper reaches of the Amazon to the beach at Ipanema. The Captain's Woman steps back to the 1930s and the legendary exploits of Brazil's own Bonnie and Clyde, Lampião and Maria Bonita. Forgotten Tigers of Rio de Janeiro and the title story, The Secret's in the Folding, revisit the age of slavery. All unfamiliar territory — to this reader, at least — yet I finished this volume feeling I'd been there, seen the destitute mother under the mango tree waiting for the fruit to fall, picked up a cashew leaf perforated in the image of the Madonna, smelled the wood-smoke and toffee-scented air by Celestina's shack, tasted the Cake to Please Mothers-in-law.

Fiona Thackeray conjures Brazil with a sensual combination of scents, flavours, flora, fauna, landscape, pitch-perfect idiom and a beady eye for human peculiarity. To read her stories is to discover not just a new corner of the world, but also a new way of looking at that world. A candle-lit vigil draws confetti-clouds of moths. A shot glass, toppled in a bar-room brawl, rolls in diminishing arcs. An old woman comes out of a rainstorm dripping like washed collards in a sieve. There is beauty here, and exoticism — to northern European eyes — but no tourist board air-brushing. Shanty town dwellers are burned out by the police. A slave's skin is marked by his mistress's urine. A celebrity magazine favourite is exposed as the former mistress of a dictator. Zoo animals in a war zone starve to death. Yet even the darkest tales are lit by glimmers of humanity.

There are sunnier stories, too. An English wife discovers her sensuality in the Brazilian heat (after an erotic epiphany involving a sewing machine!). A jealous cook is won over by the generosity of a freed slave. The janitor trapped at work while the rest of Rio celebrates Carnaval receives a reward beyond his wildest dreams. Whether poking gentle fun at provincial credulity, or chronicling the desperate hardship of northern peasant farmers, Thackeray's voice is unmistakeable: empathetic, evocative, lyrical and exquisitely observant.

Ajay Close
Author of *Official and Doubtful* and *Forspoken*

THE SECRET'S IN THE FOLDING

From behind doorjambs, suspicious eyes observed Dona Celestina come to town. Her head held high, a canvas bundle bumping her behind, creaky shoes pinching. Her stick — a hoe-handle polished by sun and years and hands — thudded the dust, leaving powdery dots. From her left hand swung a crate with feathers protruding: the two Guinea fowl who would colonise the town of Bom Jesus with their squawking progeny, and oblige Celestina with small, speckled eggs for the rest of her days. Jammed tight under this arm was a parasol.

When she'd made her patrol of our humble streets, and sat sipping water at Zé Lima's corner cafe, we watched her hoist her long frame from the chair, picking up her parasol last. Celestina headed for the river. Her crinoline hems sagged in the heat; the guinea fowl scuffled in their crude cage. Near the point where the water rumbles under the Salvador road, she set down her bundles, where the old jackfruit tree drops its seed bombs half in mud, half in the water, looping an arm over the green current. Out of sight, she took off the pinching shoes, sighing, feet splaying in the cool riverbank mud.

With a hoe-blade unrolled from her canvas bundle, jammed onto the walking stick, she cleared a patch of saplings to leave low white stumps. She began pointing the straighter bits of wood for fence stakes, mopping her brow. We heard her bitten machete ringing out and breathless reports from our little spies: local kids stalking the woods like Indians.

Using these ancient tools, Celestina spiked a fence into the ground for her two cranky birds, and a makeshift shelter for herself, the carrying canvas stretched over for a roof. Later, she could see the moon through it, and a fair few stars. In the rainy months, a symphony of leaks puddled her floor, though she never cared, splashing through with a duck's insouciance.

It was rainy season when she first came provisioning, not long after she'd put up her hut, and no doubt when she could no longer stretch out whatever supplies she brought with her. Past the saddler's she paced, gingerly in those comfortless shoes, accustomed by now to staring locals. Rain pelted her head; a perpetual baptism, but she never hurried. The parasol stayed crooked under her arm. Madalena and I watched — and wondered.

The Rural Supplies Store was first to attend Bom Jesus' newest resident. She needed rope to lash a hurdle door for her shack. Next she came creaking towards us. There was only Dona Marinete in the shop with her maid, clucking over her maize flour order, lingering, in hope of gossip.

On the threshold Celestina stopped, dripping like washed collards in a sieve. She inclined her brow towards dumbstruck Dona Marinete, whose jaw dropped.

"*Bom dia.* What weather!" I greeted her.

Celestina withdrew the parasol from its tight place and thrust it on the counter. "A bushel of flour, I should like, please. And a good three pounds of sugar, Senhor."

She looked me proudly in the eye, yet called me Senhor as a maid might. I wondered how to address her — Senhora was grand for a black woman in old crinolines. While I weighed sugar, my other two customers bewailed the downpour, eager chins tilted at Celestina. She said nothing, and set her provisions by the door.

Nodding at the rain, she declared, "I'll collect it later."

Dona Marinete opened her mouth, but Celestina spun on her heel, and departed, picking through the terracotta wash.

Plucking at the maid's sleeve, Dona Marinete left too, hitching billowing skirts clear of the mud. Maria tottered behind, struggling to keep a sun-faded black parasol positioned over her mistress's bouncing curls.

Not two hours later, Celestina returned. "Pssst! Senhor! I think the Good Lord's sparing us more rain. Maybe I'll take that flour now." She smiled, less guarded.

"O! I haven't had a minute to check on those clouds!"

"No matter, weather's fine." Tutting, she forbad any fuss, arranging her sack-load. The rain had stopped, it was true, but iron-red puddles held reflections of fat clouds.

"Maybe not for long, mind."

"I'll take it!" she shuddered impatiently. Like a strapping farmhand she was off down the track, shouldering the sack.

Bent double — the first fat rain-spots already blotching her headscarf — she didn't see the two Policia Militar closing rank ahead, like a grey wall. "Errands for your Mistress, lady?"

She balanced the sack and fumbled in her skirts for her Emancipation Papers. The policemen scrutinised them, holding them as if contaminated. They spat, and left. I watched her go, every humiliated step, the rain steadily turning her flour to paste.

Our new customer awoke with her birds next day to set a fire and cook up sweet-corn puddings, sticky pumpkin hearts and passion fruit patties. Late morning, she appeared in the square, setting her wares on upturned crates, a cautious two feet under the gables of the town hall. Business was slow at first — she hadn't counted on the suspicious nature of Bom Jesus folks. Still, we were a people deprived of sweetmeats, save the dusty old biscuits in my shop storeroom. Gradually, customers were seduced by smells, sampled her special recipes and were smitten.

Around Bom Jesus, Celestina's economical conversing had whetted curiosities. When pressed she'd say she came from "the countryside". Quite unawares, she had driven the ladies from the big houses wild with inquisitiveness — to the brink of losing their refined ways. Dona Serena had even ridden the sugar cane barge as far as Dores, under the guise of "a vigil against cane pilfering", ogling, from the deck, Celestina's patch. All to verify whether she really did sit straddling a rock, "fishing and chewing tobacco like a man" as our spying young folks had reported. The gaps in her story, like honey traps, invited the town's talkers to fall in and wallow in preposterous fantasies. She was a witch from the forest in the North, or mother of "Saçi", the peg-legged rascal who soured milk and set plagues on bean crops. She was, tattled washer-girls from Cascudo's coffee plantation, an African Queen, owing to her stately rhythm of walking. (I put that down to calluses from those shoes).

The Senhoras of the plantations, over afternoon coffee, dismissed such fairy tales.

Eyes narrowed knowingly.

"She's blacker than the grains in this coffee pot, dears," they conspired, spitting crumbs of cornmeal cake over dainty cups.

14

"Must be descended from those shipped over from Africke, a Gold Coast slave baby, ladies."

She'd run away, perhaps, or bought her freedom. It didn't matter much — they knew where she was from.

Dona Celestina stayed ahead of the gossips. Her divine wares soon brought out-of-hours callers to the riverbank. A sign appeared in childish script:

CAKES, PIES & CONFECKSIONERY
Any request considered.

Madalena said one of the boys at school painted it, with payment in pumpkin puddings. They say she'd fashioned some type of a clay oven. Soon she'd no need to go the square any more. For the inquisitive souls of Bom Jesus, it was the perfect excuse for snooping. Always ready for them — the guinea fowl raised the alarm — she'd close the door, squeeze into her shoes, and wait on the packed earth, the birds scratching around her feet. In nonchalant twos or threes, dangling empty baskets, they came. Celestina held their crumpled papers to the light filtering through the jackfruit leaves, squinting at spidery ink. Her bony fingers conjured sweet steam and ingredients in the air, slyly guessing what those scribbled notes meant. The fingertips came to pause on her chest and raindrops gathered upon the ribs of banana leaves as she memorised recipes, considered a price.

That first year, the rains never let up. Celestina came to us regularly, carrying the furled parasol, rain or shine.

Madalena asked, "Papai, why doesn't that senhora put up her parasol? She's getting all wet."

15

And I would pinch her for her insolence and send her scurrying to offer water, or a *cafezinho* to rain-mizzled Celestina.

One ceaselessly wet day, the shop got crowded — the baker's boy, two travelling salesmen, and Dona Marinete's daughters down from the Fazenda Fortuna — all sheltering from the rain. I'd set Madalena making coffee, the smell made people forget the weather. Celestina, approaching through sheets of silver, faltered a little in her stride on seeing the dampened huddle.

"*Bom dia,*" she mumbled.

I came out from the back shop to greet her.

"I'm wet, flesh and bone! My usual flour order, Senhor Joaquim," she sighed.

I felt my own daughter's insolent curiosity jumping in my throat — she was so utterly drenched that day — why did she never use the damned parasol?

It was an old thing, she was muttering, and a little fragile.

The assembled shelterers raised eyebrows at each other.

In the end, I was discreet, recommending Senhor Alois' services. "He mends everything, cages, baskets, wheels. A parasol could not be so different."

Celestina thanked me, rush, rush, and was gone. I watched her hobble towards Alois' place. They smiled and conversed as sun punched through the rain clouds. But later, when I'd despatched the last of my sheltering salesmen, the old man was bewildered by my talk of repairs. He'd taken no commission from the sweet maker. She had paid a social call, nothing more. He shrugged, clipping the last wires on Dr Limoge's stoat cages.

Our hardy *quituteira*[†] was becoming a legend. Few resisted her coconut ice pyramids, and angel babas. Soon she qualified for a bulk discount: a happy arrangement — we prospered together. On occasion, she even left the parasol with us when her load was too cumbersome.

Late one afternoon, Madalena could be seen running out to a cloud of yellow butterflies, their twitching wings mirrored in a steaming puddle. We'd just made coffee, and the trees dripped musically. I sat sipping on my peroba-wood stool, taking Celestina's parasol on my knee. The closure was a little perished but kept the canvas panels neatly furled. It hooked over the tiniest mother-of-pearl button. With a mahogany point it was a fine piece of craftsmanship, even if Celestina never used it for its intended purpose. I returned, then, to parcelling cassava meal.

Madalena was going through a dancing phase. Getting her to the schoolhouse was impossible for she would always be under the mango tree, pirouetting and stamping. She would take twigs in her hands, and spin like some little dervish. I, engrossed in balancing parcels against stout brass weights, was unaware that Madalena had tired of butterflies and spied a fine parasol to embellish her dances. With the stealth of a shadow, my impetuous daughter had taken it and gone slinking outside.

Her dainty fingers stretched the perished closure over the pearly button. The canvas folds fell looser on their spokes. She felt inside for the catch; her hand lost its way a little against raw edges of fabric. The mechanism was

---

[†] *Quituteira* — maker and street vendor of sweets and savouries

17

stiff. But with gentle force she managed to push open the radial of spokes.

Dust and ancient moth wings flew in her face. She coughed, shrieked; her mischief revealed. I came running and we stood and stared as if at long-forgotten bones. Sun filtered through thin ribbons of canvas. Between spokes, the fabric gave way to grotesque, fray-edged holes and green islands of mildew. Rust-stained threads fluttered to earth, and the rich dust of years swirled and settled, some on Madalena's nose. The canvas remnants, carefully arranged, had concealed this decrepitude. Rain came suddenly, battering our roof as Madalena stared in horror at me and then at the ravaged thing in her outstretched fist.

Try and try as we might, we could not fold the parasol's ragged panels into their former order. Whichever way we closed and rolled, decay protruded. Dislodged motes and insect fragments peppered the canvas.

My look must have been terrible when Celestina reappeared. She was breathless, rain spangling her wiry hair.

"Oh, Senhor Jo!" she called from the doorway. I came from the storeroom. "I was delayed. I believe we are due for some sunshine."

She stopped, her gaze falling on my hands. For a long moment, she looked at rain rippling the puddles. The clay-clouded water mirrored her unfurled shame. Madalena came, we tried to explain, but it was all too bare. The parasol, no sun or rain guard, was but spokes and shreds, and a lot of dust and mould besides. And we knew now why she carried it always closed. It was just a symbol, like a badge or an ostrich-feather hat. I looked at her inherited shoes, cutting weals in her ankles, and realised she'd no way to pay Alois' repair bill.

Celestina looked at her parasol, her property, holes and all. The threads had been brighter in the days when she'd carried it, intact, over the head of a mistress — days when she herself had been property, no better than an object, a tattered sunshade. Now she carried her no-good parasol to show the world she was a free woman who had belongings and that she belonged to nobody.

There were no customers then, no need for a lie, but I said it anyway. "Such a fine object. I would not, perhaps, entrust it to the local craftsmen."

At last she raised her face to meet mine. She said her words, but she knew that I understood better the graven set of her jaw and her unmoving eyes.

She spoke slowly, "So you would agree, Senhor, that it might be better to await the right class of tradesman?" She accepted my feeble offering.

I shrugged. "Yes, Celestina, it may be better to wait." We breathed out as she turned to leave.

The rains didn't stop until late February. Celestina carried her parasol for many weeks to follow, somehow re-furled to suggest ivory entirety. We tut-tutted over it without opening its folds, and she complained of how holes show up just when it rains most, as if the holes were newly appeared. The other customers shook their heads in sympathy, and we agreed that some day she would find the right person to repair it.

Later it occurred to me, with irritation, that our little charade might be bad for Senhor Alois' business. Between us we made quite a fuss, implying no craftsman was equal to the infamous parasol. People might think him incapable

19

of simple repairs. But I discovered through Madalena's eavesdropping, that Celestina was his and my best advocate, singing our praises around town.

"O Senhor Joaquim is a true connoisseur and Senhor Alois so patient with me. He knows how to treat articles of quality." And so we settled into a comfortable conspiracy.

The horsemen from the farms now rode into town a little plumper in their saddles from Celestina's cakes. The ladies sent to Rio for exotic ingredients for Celestina's blending. There was a certain air of competition amongst the big plantation houses to improve their 'secret' teatime recipes — all Celestina's, of course. She worked until she ran out of candles, later on full-moon nights. Gradually, she bought bricks to build a proper oven and cord with which to knot a hammock.

With the slow way of country girls, the young senhoritas of the plantations picked up on the fashion for the new, dainty parasols a little late. In Rio and Petropolis, Dom Pedro II was never seen without his. The royal court and the Carioca ladies had fallen for them like a fever the year before, strolling on Copacabana with tiered and lace-frilled models. It was perfect timing for us, behind the Rio folks or not, as Madalena was getting old enough to help Senhor Alois in the workshop with parasol mending and remodelling, and it kept her away from the farm-boys.

Business thrived too for Celestina. Parasol-twirling promenades were fashionably followed, in all the best houses, with coffee and cake; which vogue ignited even greater competition between the plantation houses. She baked endlessly, dreaming up 'exclusive' recipes for each Senhora's requirements. Alois and I made a deal. Next time she left the parasol with me, I'd send it over to him for secret mending. It was our great pleasure to imagine her surprise at finding the holes mysteriously gone. Until we realised: she may never open the thing. We even bet on how long it would take her to discover that she could now open her parasol without shame.

Our plan never came to be. Around that time, she hung up the parasol and it never rested on our shelf again. Perhaps — who am I to say why — respected for her craft as she was, she forgot the need to carry her badge of freedom.

The parasol was the only thing to disappear from Celestina's routine. Her crinkled smile — long accustomed to the harsh elements without benefit of canvas protection — regularly lit up our shop. She came to sip coffee and talk about business and how times were good. Thanks to her, we are the proud keepers of Matilde and Adão, whose speckled eggs provide my morning omelette and whose infernal squawks wake me at five each day.

Celestina left no heir, though her birds grieved silently. It was sullen Maria, gone to collect Dona Marinete's orange-flower cake, who found her slumped peacefully over a heap of eggshells. Don't ask me where my girl gets her notions but Madalena ran down there while they carried off the body and found that damn parasol in the shack. Cradled in the jackfruit tree, she ripped mildewed tatters from spokes and fed them to the racing river below. The bruise-coloured map of Celestina's life before Bom Jesus sucked away on the current. We worked into the small hours, under Alois' put-puttering lamp, recovering the frame in starchy fabric, fresh as Chantilly cream.

In blinding January sun we proceeded, Madalena weeping silently. From church to river, I strained my old arm holding the parasol over the coffin. Dona Celestina, like never in her life, was laid to rest shaded by the finest parasol.

TRADE SECRETS OF JANITORS

"The time has come, my friend."

A man in tight tee-shirt and denims bursts through the door marked 'Janitorial Services'.

"Where're you going looking so bonita?" his colleague asks, chewing on a toothpick, from a seat by the window.

"Shut up, Freitas. You just jealous 'cos you're spending Carnaval right here." The man in jeans throws his overalls into a laundry hamper.

"Yeah, you lucky bastard." Freitas lifts his chin from the palm of his hand, slides his elbow lethargically off the counter. "It's gonna be a scream. I should be strutting it down that damn Sambódromo right now, having the time of my life."

"You got the short straw this year, baby. I almost feel sorry for you. I says to King Size, I says, 'This rota's cruel, man. Freitas lives for Carnaval.' You know what that *puto* says to me, man?"

Freitas shrugs.

"He says, 'Pretinho, life is cru-el.' You believe that?"

"What an asshole." They laugh.

"Life is cru-el." Pretinho apes the supervisor again. "The whole o' Rio knows Freitas drums every year with the Beija-Flor Samba School — everybody except King Size."

"He knows alright; he rota'd me tonight out of pure spite. His old lady parades with the Caprichosos. Messing with the rota, that's his little Carnaval sabotage. It won't help their sorry chances, but, thanks to that fat pig, I'm sitting this year out."

23

"No kidding? The mean bastard. Whole hospital rota's messed up, though," says Pretinho, serious now. "Hardly nobody on duty."

"S'the same every year." Freitas waves a hand, dismissive. "Skeleton staff, everybody takes leave."

"Still," Pretinho flicks his towel towards Freitas, "better hope no serious shit happens."

"Nothin' gonna happen — just three days of sitting on my ass while the rest of the country parties."

"Yeah, getting laid, dancing... bad luck, man." Pretinho wiggles his hips in anticipation of the samba moves he'll be making later. "Okay, gotta go."

"Hey, turn on the set there. The parade must be starting. I wanna see my Angel of angels." Pretinho reaches up to the dial on a small TV.

"Staying loyal to Goddess Luma then; still believe in angels?"

"*Sim Senhor*! I'd follow that ass anywhere."

Freitas remembers the day Luma da Silveira returned to rehearsals. Each year for the last seven, during the weeks between Christmas and Carnaval, he'd admired the sway of her curves to the sambistas' rhythms from his vantage point near the back of the rehearsal hall.

"No picture. This thing's finally done for." Pretinho thumps the TV, to no effect. "This is your lucky shift, Freitas. Hey, catch you later."

"*Tchau.*"

Pretinho's tuneless whistle recedes along the corridor. Freitas sighs. He opens the window, leaning out in the direction of the parade-ground. There, in marquees, sambistas are assembling in small clutches, like mythical creatures in their feathers and glitter, looping arms around

24

each other, muttering prayers. TV stars and models huddle with cleaners and caretakers: equally glamorous, equally scared. He hears the announcer's voice booming like a distant storm over Guanabara Bay. Freitas pictures King Size, a leering toad on the margins of spotlight pools, close enough to touch the dancers' headdresses, babbling like a fool. He grabs the Duty Rota, crumples it into a ball and lobs it hard at the TV. Just then, his radio crackles.

"Freitas? You read me?"

He twiddles the channel button. "Freitas, over."

"You'll like this job." A woman's voice, Alma, probably, that wisecrack from the control booth. "There's a little *vomitada* in the waiting area, Floor One. Can you take care of it?"

"No place I'd rather be," mutters Freitas, before squeezing the button on his handset. "On my way."

He pulls a mop and bucket from the closet and swings into the corridor. Two nurses get in the service elevator, giggling, full of plans for the holiday. Freitas wants to loop his arm inside theirs, like he'd never seen the Duty Rota, and walk out into the night air, towards the sparkle and heat of the parade. As the lift bumps to a halt, he knows that would be desperate.

"Kiss kiss, *tchau*, *tchau*." The nurses smile and wave, leaving only their perfume behind, filling the lift with the scent of abandonment as the doors close.

Floor One. Around twenty casualties are seated between pillars that span the central area. The seats on one side are empty, a soupy liquid splattered over the floor. People are bunched up in the other rows. Freitas' heart sinks. As he gets closer, a sour smell chokes his nostrils. He leaves the mop and goes to get water.

25

He turns the tap forcefully, water thunders into the zinc bucket. Finding a bottle of Chlorox under the sink, he squirts a liberal jet into the water. Caustic steam stings his eyes, but it smells clean, at least. Freitas shakes out a cloth and begins wiping. An old woman shakes her head slowly, tut-tutting. It's not clear whether she sympathises — frowning on the kind of people who soil hospital floors — or whether she disapproves of Freitas' cleaning methods.

Bernadete, an orderly, comes to replenish the coffee flasks.

"Freitas? You didn't rehearse all those months to be cleaning floors tonight, huh?"

Freitas morosely swirls his mop in the bucket, his eyes dark with unspoken resentment. Bernadete puts the flasks on a table. "Never mind, sweetie. I don't care for all that razzmatazz anyway."

"Dona Bernadete, what's not to like? The crazy costumes, everyone smiling — and you don't find beautiful mulatas like that anywhere but Rio. You got to at least like it out of patriotism."

Two men in dishevelled bridal gowns, outlandish wigs and gold face-paint arrive. One clutches his head, the other fusses.

"Too showy for me." Bernadete wags a chubby finger, raising her brow meaningfully towards the wounded bride: he's wailing now, a casualty of Carnaval. She saunters off with the empty flasks.

Freitas shakes his head. The cords of the mop fan out in grey water. Emptying the bucket over the sink, he hums the Beija-Flor anthem and tries to escape, to the night that was meant to be: marching in dazzling white with spangled epaulettes, a Bright Comet in Beija-Flor's 'Parade of

Celestial Bodies'. Drumbeats reverberate through his chest, Luma's heavenly body in the distance, sweating, sparkling: a night of perfect happiness.

He slouches back towards base, past wards where glassy-eyed patients watch the Samba Schools' progress on TV — the only colour in rooms of bleached linen. Freitas knows it's somehow wrong to enter the wards just for the chance to see some parade coverage, but tells himself that anyone stuck in hospital over Carnaval would be glad of some company. He knocks, pointing through the glass door at the rubbish bin in the first room. Smiling, he enters just in time to see Caprichosos School exiting the Sambódromo. Rain is beginning to fall. The camera scans the crowd, sheltering under plastic capes. Patients look at Freitas askance as he lingers a little longer than is necessary for emptying bins, his eyes sidling towards the bright TV screen.

Beija-Flor is announced. Freitas can't stop his feet twitching in the patterns they have danced so many times. Luma, a scandal of red sequins, sails into the arena on top of a spinning globe on the first float. An aerial view shows her passing under the concrete archway of the Sambódromo, her arms spread to greet the crowd. Raindrops glisten on her skin.

Freitas is called to Casualty. Cursing under his breath, he hurries along to the treatment cubicles. He finds Dr Eduardo Ribeiro attending a gringo with nasty cuts. The gringo's teary girlfriend stands by his side. Freitas likes Ribeiro — one of the few who treat him well.

The doctor looks up. "You too? Now I know I've a lifetime of bad karma to make up for, but why are you here tonight? They say you're the soul of Carnaval."

27

"*É, Doutor,* number one tambour, second bloco, that's where I should be. I'd really like to know what evil forces arranged this Duty Rota too."

Ribeiro laughs, tightening a stitch in the male patient's eyebrow.

The patient speaks: faltering Portuguese, heavy German accent. "We were so much excited about Carnaval. Then these little guys offer to take pictures for us. They ran off with our camera."

Freitas, bagging up bloodied gauze, exchanges knowing looks with the doctor.

The German goes on. "I chased, but out of nowhere a guy with broken bottle comes. Such a shame — all our pictures of the parade."

"That's the reality of Rio, I'm afraid. Though it's much safer than it was," says the doctor. "My father always says Carnaval's the only thing that works in Brazil: starts bang on time, parades go in perfect formation: they lose points for starting late."

"That's true," Freitas laughs.

The German girl chips in. "It's amazing what those people achieve — such beautiful costumes and trucks, and they're all poor people. From the slums!"

The doctor winks.

Freitas smiles, adding, "Brazilians don't have much but we've got certain natural talents — rhythm for Carnaval, a knack for kicking a ball..."

Ribeiro grins, snapping off his latex gloves. "Yeah, things could be worse, Freitas. Miss the World Cup and you wait four years. At least with Carnaval there's always next year."

"Yeah, not the end of the world."

But Luma is threatening to retire next year and Carnaval may never be the same. Ribeiro slaps him on the back as he leaves, telling the Germans to take care.

Freitas thinks maybe now he can catch a glimpse of the Beija-Flor finale. His radio hisses.

"Honeybunch, another good one for you. Damsel in distress down in Admissions. There's a dog involved." Alma's voice is smirking.

Freitas' first thought is a pile of dog shit, or a foaming Pit-Bull hanging from someone's arm. He doesn't feel brave as he pushes the trolley from the treatment room, making a parting thumbs-up sign to the Germans. In the stairwell window, Rio's misty morning silhouette is emerging. A pink slice of Flamengo harbour is visible at the end of the street. In the distance, the Sugar Loaf is tangled in cable-car wires that droop into the fog. Freitas takes a deep breath and pushes through the doors.

No smell of dog-mess, and no gnashing or growling: instead a slight woman in her seventies clutching a poodle. She's been crying, mascara tracking her crinkly cheeks. Dressed for exercise: huge tortoiseshell shades propped on a 'Skol' baseball cap, gold training bootees, wrinkled skin sags over the waistband of her running tights; she sits in a wheelchair, blood oozing from her knee. A nurse perches nearby.

The poodle barks as Freitas gets closer. "*Alô* Senhora... what happened here?" The poodle grimaces, revealing comical tiny teeth.

The Senhora's red eyes peep from beneath the bill of her cap. "They won't let Tatá stay. There's nowhere for him to go." She begins to sob again.

The nurse rolls her eyes and explains in a tone of polite but stretched patience. "Dona Mariella was hit by a roller-blader on her morning constitutional. She needs stitches and X-rays, but little Tatá here can't come along."

"He's very clean — he had his bath at the parlour yesterday." The woman's voice rises a pitch or two. Tatá turns and licks her chin.

Freitas catches himself staring: she's somehow familiar. "What a handsome little chap. Hey, Tatá..." He risks a finger under the poodle's chin. Its ears prick up and nervous little eyes widen. "You know, I think he's worried about his owner." Freitas looks into Dona Mariella's eyes over the poodle's white fuzz.

Her chin puckers and she dabs tears with a shaky hand. "He's shocked, maybe even concussed. It was a big chap. Fifty kilometres per hour at least, straight into us."

"Senhora, you must be hurting. How about you let me take care of Tatá? After the doctor's seen you, I'll bring him right back and you can take him to the vet."

"But Tatá's not used to anyone else. He's a nervous boy."

The nurse chimes in, "Just for an hour while we examine you?"

The patient surveys her knee, swelling beneath torn leopard-print Lycra, then ruffles Tatá's curly head. Turning, she nudges the dog towards Freitas over the arm of the wheelchair. He grasps Tatá awkwardly — one leg gets doubled back. The dog yelps.

"Oh, *querido!*" Dona Mariella panics.

Freitas adjusts the bony white leg. "I've got him now," he smiles. The dog looks stoically ahead, paws paddling the air. The nurse begins manoeuvring the wheelchair, Dona Mariella craning her neck around.

"Be good, Tatá."

Freitas waves. "Don't you worry, Senhora."

Upstairs, Freitas sets Tatá on the floor. The poodle begins to sniff around, never taking his eyes off his new minder. The caretaker crosses his arms, watching. He remembers his dinner, uneaten on the counter, and reaches over to retrieve a piece of beef fat from the foil tin. The dog is instantly at his feet, looking hopeful.

"Now we're friends, huh?" Freitas holds the fat behind his back for a moment and the dog sits down in sombre obedience. "Who got the best Samba anthem in Rio? Eh, doggy? Bark if it's Beija-Flor."

The poodle looks back, blinking. Freitas shrugs and gives him the fat. Tatá chews laboriously.

"You be good now. Don't piss on this floor, or you've had it, y'hear?" He can't help but smile at the forlorn figure on matchstick legs, dwarfed by the furniture, cocking his head as Freitas leaves.

Later, Freitas finds Dona Mariella in Orthopaedics. "Senhora, *tudo bem*? Little chap's all settled. He says take as long as you need." He winks. The woman raises her head from the pillow.

"God bless you," she says.

Freitas has a light bulb to change in the Scrub Room, Floor Three, and a leaking toilet to fix on Two. When he finally returns to his room, the poodle comes to sniff him. The wastepaper bin has been upended and a pale trickle meanders from a plastic bottle onto the floor.

"You little pest! Got a taste for Limonada, eh?" Freitas pats the dog's tousled fringe as he cleans the spillage. He

31

spends a half-hour trying to teach the bemused Tatá to raise his right paw for Fluminense football team, his left for Flamengo, but eventually the dog goes to lie in the corner, sighing. Several ambulances are approaching the hospital. Their sirens combine in ear-splitting howls. Freitas looks out from his little window: the sky is losing its rosy intensity now. The melancholy cloud of Carnaval night has lifted, leaving arcs of peach and iron stretching over the city. In the street below, yellow acacia leaves pasted to the pavements by the night rains are like pages from a scrapbook. Freitas wonders if Beija-Flor really have won again and everyone gone to The Armadillo's Den to celebrate. He imagines King Size, probably drunk and rueful by now, draped around the wife, a pitiful mix of lechery and commiseration.

Tatá raises an eyebrow, suddenly alert. Slow footsteps echo in the corridor. Freitas stretches, rubs his chin and checks his watch: the saddest shift is nearly over. Three raps on the door startle him. Tatá barks, already half way across the room.

"*Entra*," Freitas calls. Silence. He walks over and yanks the door. In the windowless corridor, a woman in an overcoat waits, smiling. Her hair hangs in damp loops, her dangerous red sequins are subdued now, glinting between the folds of her coat. Smudged make-up gives her eyes a vulnerable air. Tatá, wagging his tail, is jumping at Luma's ankles.

"You helped my mother." Her hands pull his face close. Her lips press against his cheek. "Thank you."

Her eyes narrow. "Hey," she says, "you're one of ours, right? Beija-Flor drumming corps — I recognise you."

Freitas' jaw feels frozen shut, his blood surging where she kissed him. He smiles, almost manages to nod.

"Why weren't you there?" Luma shakes her head a little, incredulous that he could miss the climax of all those months of rehearsal.

"Oh...an act of God, I guess." Freitas, surprised he can talk at all, is making no sense. "I was needed here."

"You sure were. Shame, though. You know we won?"

"'Course we did." He smiles. He had known, kind of.

"It's a real pity you missed it, but I'm so glad you were here for *Mamãe*. Without you, I..." She looks down at the wire-framed wings dangling from her forearm, damp from rain, though still glittery. "Well, you'll get your reward in heaven."

"I already did," Freitas grins.

Luma scoops up Tatá and leaves, turning back once to smile over her shoulder. Outside in the acacia branches, kiskadees announce the new day with riotous screams. More ambulances arrive, drowning out the birds. In a daze, the imprint of Luma's lips warm on his cheek, her strange scent of glitter-paint and lilies still with him, Freitas hears the impatient sirens and knows there's been a major incident. He remembers Pretinho's worried face, 'better hope no serious shit happens'. He had planned to walk home by the Sambódromo, through the lost sequins and discarded paper flowers, perhaps pick up a souvenir. Now he realises they may need him here; it's Carnaval after all, and they are short-staffed. Freitas heads back down to Casualty. His feet, squeaking on the linoleum, follow a familiar rhythm, his keys bounce on his thigh and he's singing, gently, the Samba of the Celestial Bodies.

WATERCOLOURS

May's hair — strawberry blond streaked with silver — flicked upwards. Her sandy freckles looked dark as cracked pepper in the shade of her famous straw hat. She sat in the stern looking back over the water, churned to white in our wake. While I scratched and reddened in clouds of mosquitoes, she remained delicate, porcelain in white linen and khaki. I feel guilty now, for moaning about my blossoming bites while she poured her soul into her sketches.

Her subject was the formidable Victoria Regia water lily, strung out like bloated frogspawn on the wide wash. Crinkled dinner plates of chlorophyll, reluctant to give up their secret structure to May and her tablets of colour. For days she sat in her straw-brimmed shadow, patiently constructing the stubborn curves from every angle, sweeping pencils over thick pages to the engine's unremitting drone. If she sighed in exasperation, I never heard it.

I remember how I was fooled by her delicate ways as we drank tea at Gatwick, papery fingers looped around the cup.

"Milk, dear?"

May was Mum's age — would she bear up in the Tropics? Then in Manaus, seeing her barter with the boat guys while I, gesticulating dumbly, failed to fend off over-attentive coconut sellers. She spoke fluent Portuguese from

Institute trips with George to sketch flowering trees of São Paulo. She was an old hand.

May prowled over the boat, poking at spots of rust, jiggling loose cables. She ignored the owner's squinting look that mocked, and questioned him ruthlessly; her shrewd and steady voice belied by brittle blonde looks. Eventually she struck a deal, stepping onto the harbour side, graceful as a visiting grandee.

We loaded our stuff: bundled clothes thrown like hay bales, art materials passed as crown jewels over the muddy spit of Amazon sucking between boat and steps. The engine rumbled into life, whisking up bubbles to the water's oily surface and, coughing, took us out into the middle of the brutal green flow.

My companion seemed serene then, making herself at home on our guttering boat. She roped her hammock facing west so she might watch birds at sunset. I was kind of edgy — something about the weird ticking noises of hidden insects in the reeds, the river's false tranquillity — lazy ripples concealing murderous currents and muscular reptiles. The cook brewed afternoon coffee, and we sipped it listlessly, watching the remnants of slums peter out on the banks. May looked faintly imperious, reclining with her dainty cup and hat, reflections dancing over her face. The captain's gruff voice in short staccato phrases interrupted our languor. May called back in melodious Portuguese, sounding like a native. Again, the captain in short serious bursts.

May replied laughing, wafting her hand. "He's worried about Indians," she smiled. "In Manaus they love telling stories of forest savages. I told him they always invited us to tea."

May's leisured air was replaced by animated concentration as we opened botanical guides to plan our work. The Institute had requested a series of plates of the Victoria Regia varieties, and at various different stages of growth. The lilies were a great challenge: something elusive in their veiny flatness that May relished. My job would be to catalogue her work — in between times, sketching the riverbank vegetation, a watercolour diary of the trip for my end-of-year assignment. In the process I planned to learn all I could from the Grand Dame of botanical art.

If nights in a hammock swarmed by mosquitoes are harder on older bones, May never showed it. She rose at six each day and painted till 11.30, then after lunch again until sundown. Pages leafed to the deck in loose piles around her feet. Salvador, at the wheel, turned out to be an obliging sort, steering us to where he knew we would find dense miles of lily pads. He dropped anchor for hours wherever May requested, swinging in his hammock with one eye always on the banks, until the rubbery dinner-plate leaves had been lined and coloured many times over. The boat creaked in silty ripples, only sylvan squawks and crooning marked the passing of the day. Sometimes Salvador and May would get down the peeling little rower and slip between the green discs to slice a sub-aqueous bulb, or a pale leaf shoot only half unfurled. My book was filling up too, with the spikes and twisting greens of riverbank trees in their dense, tangled ranks.

Back at St Martins we'd had a whistle-stop tour of the basic drawing media, and the watchword was experimental. We scribbled in charcoal and ink, pencil and pastels and we daubed mud and coffee dregs on the page too. Now I wallowed in watercolour, soaking up everything May told me. She showed me how flat images will be if you rush in with dark shades first. I watched colour swim into place as she painted 'into the wet,' her skies the colour of fish scales, areas left unpainted bringing water-scenes alive, final, inky details etched over colour in her impossibly light hand — like life, only more beautiful. She made lines bold, then delicate, and perfectly parallel with sweeps that had me despairing at my own thick-boned fingers.

We ate rice, beans and fried fish for lunch. Fruit, too, when the cook spied something good ripening. I watched him go ashore with his basket, foraging among the thick, drooping foliage and I only relaxed when he was onboard with us again. In the long evenings, I sorted and dated her paintings, rifling through field guides for variety and sub-species names. Salvador and the cook played cards with much shouting, and we all drank beer, chilled in the rusty fridge. I imagined May sipping Calvados at home, but she downed the beer gladly. Everything she did was dignified. She even mourned with dignity. It was twenty years of married life with George and many painting trips along the way. He had suffered for many months — an illness that wrung the life out of him before finally letting him go. I think I would have run through the streets in hysterical fury, or become a bitter old lush. May kept her chin up at the funeral and warmly thanked everyone for their kindness. So said Mum, who took the call in the front office, and went along to the wake. May was teaching again in two days. Soon after, I supposed, rather than ruminating on the harshness of life, her thoughts had turned to continuing alone in the work she'd done with George. As summer term rolled on, a notice appeared, advertising her expedition with space for a Research Assistant.

"We had dinner at the Consulate in '96," said May. "The Halls were great friends of ours. They showed us the most fascinating albums full of tribal people. George managed to paint a few live portraits, but the tribes are almost all gone now."

I shuddered a little.

"There's a chap works for the government. Bit of a maverick — trying to reach the remaining tribes and forewarn them, you know, about our strange ways, before less scrupulous types come across them. There have been some bloody clashes with loggers and so on, blundering across groups they don't understand." She smiled, sighing.

I realised what a poor substitute I must be for George as a travelling mate, with my phrasebook Portuguese and my utter ignorance of indigenous people and botany. Of course, May never gave me any sign that she might think that.

She'd reached a phase in her work where the common varieties were covered. Now she wanted the rare ones. Salvador swung the boat around, reluctantly, to enter a tributary where May travelled before with George; where two rivers meet in muddy swirls but do not mix. The pale Rio Solimões danced coy whirlpools between the Rio Negro's black fingers. The waters tangled but neither river would yield to blend with the other. May was received at tribal villages like an old friend and, around campfires, daintily chewing on nameless meats, she would interrogate gap-toothed fishermen about the lilac lily and the rare yellow. Salvador shrugged grudgingly at May's requested stops; he tended to stay onboard. The heat intensified as the river threaded thinner into the forest. Shirts clung and my hammock was always sweat-damp. I slapped at mosquitoes in irritable rhythms.

"The light here is so hard."

My mentor knew exactly what I meant. The sun, despite seeming distant and veiled by heavy cloud, bleached the colours out of everything. When it seemed we had passed the last habitations on earth, ready to putter upstream into oblivion, we spotted a small settlement. May thought it could be a tribal group she'd met before who had since moved. Children, splashing in the shallows, hushed as we approached and yellow butterflies spun like confetti on a whimsical breeze. We anchored in the shade of bamboo stands, and Salvador rowed with May to talk with the villagers, compact and red as mud.

May returned with a fierce light in her eyes. Along a tiny tributary, the villagers had told her, we would find her lilies.

"Our boat is too broad, though — would you mind going ahead with Salvador for a few days?"

We had to deliver promised medicine to another village. Salvador tried to stop her, tried to convey something dark to her with his eyes while the tribes-people watched, unblinking. She smiled patiently at his concern. My mind slalomed between May's attitude to these warnings as the silly prejudices of town folk, and a deeper unease that seemed to come from everywhere and nowhere — the varnished sheen of the river, the dull silver of mudbanks, the ticking sounds of the forest. We left her drawing stick-men in the sand with the children.

Salvador frowned silently as he steered upstream. Two days took us to the village, dilapidated and silent, save for sawing cricket song. We waited with the anti-malarials at the shore. For half an hour: no movement, just the feeling of being watched. Then two young men came out, weapons tied on twine from their hips, their hair cut pudding-bowl style. They yanked their heads in interrogative motions downstream, asking Salvador to explain who we were. They were slow to remember George and May's visits. Edging forward a little, they accepted the boxes, retreating then to a mouldy longhouse. The place remained still, like a sick room. We moored there for the night, and headed back at dawn.

The sky blushed, next evening, as we neared the spot where the children and yellow butterflies had danced. I was painting out in front. The birds made a great fuss at that hour, fretting and twittering as the sun slid low. I wished May were with me, exclaiming into her binoculars. Salvador was stone-faced behind the wheel. I emptied my jar of bruise-coloured water, and went to stand by him.

"What was the matter?" I asked.

He ignored me, bringing the speed right down.

We were level with a clearing of flattened earth and the white wounds of cut stems. Salvador was breathing hard, sweat collecting in the creases of his neck. His black eyes would not meet mine, glowering under the brow bone.

I told him, "This must be where May visited last time, where the villagers used to live before."

He was shaking his head slowly. The boat puttered forwards, and the cook came to the deck. They talked fast, knowing I wouldn't understand. The cook paled, blew out cheeks of air.

"Are we lost? Have we come too far?"

They did not answer. Doubt and dread prickled my scalp. We slugged along for half an hour or more, infinite in my sense of time. My heart beat painfully, as if I'd run up a mountain.

With a terrible lurch, the boat veered towards the right bank; the engine rasped and scraped. Salvador fought with the wheel, bringing us abruptly round. He scrambled for the rower, refusing to meet my eyes. I helped him hoist it, all the time searching his face in anger and fear. I turned to clamber down, and then saw the white linen among the reeds. Hollow and haunted, her face stared from a circle of green water.

"May! My God. Hold on!" Her eyes, squeezing from their sockets, stared past us to some hideous vision. Weed lapped at her neck, sticking there like torturer's wires. Her lips were ashen and blistered. At the landing where children and butterflies had met us before, her hat bobbed in the shallows.

Getting her on board was hell; she was rigid, all slippery with riverweed. Between the three of us, we laid her on deck. Salvador turned the hose to pass a clear trickle over her swollen lips. Green-flecked river water slid from the corner of her mouth; the cook left. I was breathing hard, as if I could breathe for her too. Salvador and I took turns at pumping her ribcage. She was stiff — and cold. My arms were rubbery-weak. Water squelched through linen, up between my fingers. Her delicate ribs felt they might crush like bird's bones under my palms, the skin of her cheeks now the horrific lilac of rare lilies. I heard the cook retching.

Salvador stopped; he pulled at the crook of my arm. He was saying, "Finished, finished."

Tears slid down my face.

The journey back was unbearably silent and slow. I hardly slept, swinging next to May's empty hammock. She lay below deck, wrapped in tarpaulin, like a prize catch. The men were mute, only mosquito whines keeping me company as I stared down at the silky water churning. Her face stared back at me from between lily pads and riverweed. My questions fell, unanswered, like pebbles to the riverbed — did she have any warning that friendship had hardened into something else? What did they do with her camera, her brushes? Did she ever see her yellow lily?

Back in Manaus, the city was stewing. I sweated hours in the morgue, and afterwards the police Delegacia. Later I waited in the travel office, arranging to send May home. Then more hours, patiently explaining to the British Consul by telephone. A cocktail of plant toxins had caused asphyxiation, said the lab report. A police team were sent upriver to investigate, though Manaus's locals already had their own theories. I tried to finish May's work: made copies of her drawings to send to the Institute in São Paulo, enclosing a note saying that she died doing what she loved best. The originals I packed to bring back to St Martins.

Lethargic fans on the Post Office ceiling wrap me in hot air like sugar spinning in a candyfloss machine. I spend my time in the queue trying to forget, and yet trying to remember, to understand why she died. Finally, a flat-faced man calls me to a booth. He tapes and date stamps the poster tube over and over, his tongue pressed between his lips. He fills forms with smudgy carbon in between that stains his yellow Correios-Mail shirt.

"Receipt — *RECIBO, POR FAVOR,*" I stammer, "and insurance — *SEGUROS,* please, *FAVOR.*" He nods.

By the opera house, I sip coffee at a grimy table, ignored by waiters. Flies dance among spilt sugar grains. Salvador finds me there. He sits down, uninvited, looking at his hands. In words and gestures he begins to say something.

That the Indians are bad people; that they know too much about plants. He shakes his head at these two facts. I object: they were her friends, from before. He wags his finger impatiently. The locals have heard on the grapevine, he insists, gesturing around us at the city. He points to his dental fillings — dark gold — and to his wedding ring. He is making digging motions now. Then "bang, bang," gun shots. The whole charade is lost on me. But, undeterred, he repeats it with a few words, and gradually I get it.

A gold mining crew setting up camp, deep inland: city-boys — a little jumpy. Nearby, a small tribe of native people: living quietly, but a little close for comfort. When they venture out to hunt for meat, the miners lose their cool, misinterpreting the hunters' intentions. Gunfire: pre-emptory strikes are heard, drawing more villagers, armed and defensive, to the scene, heightening the city-boys' panic. Five fat fingers; Salvador's splayed hand represents the only ones to escape the bullets, the last of their kind. Five lonely forest folk arrive seeking refuge at the village where we'd left May. Eyes blaze indignation over a fire, and fish are left half-eaten as liquor mingles with fear and hatred. Fierce dancing begins and by dawn, young men are sullenly whittling wood into arrowheads, gathering and pounding potent plants, rolling the arrow-tips in deadly green paste. In this bitter new light, May, returning in the narrow boat with her straw hat and paintings, is just a symbol: a mocking reminder of rich incomers' fake solidarity with indigenous peoples, and what they will do when push comes to shove. As the villagers plus five pack up to move on, the woman in white linen is the start of retaliation for the shootings inland. Her stricken form floats in the reeds. Five in the lead move silently along trails, towards the gold-miners' camp. There are friendships and friendships.

Salvador sits in silence for a long while then leaves, patting my shoulder. Tears disperse coffee grounds in the bottom of my cup, and I head for the river one last time. The brown water sloughs by, its flow unchanged by gossip and slaughter, spilled pigments and lost tribes.

MANGO

The threat of callous heat was already swelling in the air as a young mother and her baby walked in the shade of white walls. Vália stopped silently by the heavy gates, 7.50 a.m. At 8.00 a.m., the noisy unlocking, the guard's unhappy recognition. She looked back at him like yesterday's ghost. His reluctant eyes conceded and with a sigh he stepped aside to let her in.

The car park at this hour was empty. Great trees spread their boughs, throwing generous shade. Back on the hill where she used to live, the trees were all cut to make room. The tin roof drank up sun all day like a basking dragon, breathing back all the heat at night. Sweat crept from every pore as, twisting in the sheets, she kept her weight off the parts that hurt. She never slept to the end of dreams under that roof. And Luiz, rankly stewing beside her, could sleep through the Eternal Fire. A blessing, some would say, but Vália saw it was his weak point.

Beneath the old mango in the centre of the car park was a bench. It would be her place again today. Shifting Joaquim onto her knee, she let her breath out slowly and rearranged the cloths he was wrapped in. He opened his eyes for just a moment.

A cleaner, polishing fingerprints from the brass of the public doorway, eyed her suspiciously. Vália looked away. The guard came from unlocking the ladies' lavatories, crunching on the pebbly path.

"There's no wind today, Senhora. You won't see any mango fall from this tree." He was standing over her, hands on hips.

She sniffed and looked down, tweaking the cloth over Joaquim's cheek.

The guard shifted his weight impatiently to the other leg. "Of all the places with mango trees in town..." Another sigh. "We close at six, you have to go then. And don't bother anyone." With a rough flick of his key bunch he paced back towards the gate.

Under the tree was peaceful. The Museu de Arte Sacra was an old building. Its trees too were old, forgiving shelters. Many people came just to kneel in the Museum chapel and meet Father Timoteo, famed for his benedictions and compassion. Vália knew it was a special place, holy and cleansing. The best thing was the peace. Where she had come from, so much noise and tension. Always some fight or siren, shots sometimes, Pagode music and mothers screaming. Here the tall white walls deadened the traffic drone, and people spoke in low respectful voices. Here, at least for a while, she was safe. No one would look for a slum girl at the Museum.

She had put her faith in God. There was no choice of refuge for someone like her. But God would provide for her, if she waited for Him long enough. He would draw the white walls in close and she could vanish in the big city. He would stir up a wind for a mother and her baby in need. No big storm, just a few gusts to make the branches sway. And a fruit would fall. It would be her mango, not stolen, but freely given to her in a public place from a sheltering tree.

Spying the glossy leaves above the wall two nights ago, the idea had come to her. Such a tall tree, a mature one. All she could see were the higher branches. Maybe it was a vision — she liked to think so — a sign for her to go where she would be cared for, to this peaceful, pure place, out of sight. Craning back her neck, she looked up into the sturdy canopy, a sooty green and sunlight rash. She could disappear in its shade. Bending down the outer twigs, fat mangoes, green with blushing bottoms. She knew how the flesh would yield to her bite, the fibres lacing her teeth, the juice soaking her chin and neck. Smoothing the baby's cheek, nodding, she had only to wait in faith.

Gliding quietly into the car park, a shiny car with tinted windows. A man in damp linen stepped out to open the door for a woman with a handbag. She took his arm with a crinkly smile, and they strolled to the entrance. Válin pulled her shirt to hide a rosette of dirty looking bruises, suddenly ashamed. The woman's lilac blouse sleeves fluttered half way down her forearms revealing fine, liver-blotched wrists, like a leopardess. A rumour of flowery perfume trailed her. Behind this, Válin thought she could smell smoke, but she couldn't tell from where.

Joaquim was waking now, wrinkling up his face as the hot day seeped in on his lullaby dreams. His eyelids were smooth like fallen petals as he slumbered. Now, folded back deep into the sockets, they let in hard times and hunger. He stared silently into her face, worked his gums, switched focus up into the mango branches. He was, for a moment, bewitched by pendulous fruits and patchwork shadows. Then the crease across his nose returned, and the first faltering sputters of his cry. Soon his mouth tautened to a vent, bewailing his empty stomach.

Her nipple stoppered his anguish; the tight little mouth softened as milk flowed to his belly. Vál400 hunched shyly over her son and looked behind. The guard pretended not to stare.

By noon the car park was crowded. The leopard woman had left; families and couples had been and gone. Now a few people sat on benches and walls. Bodies drifted from one scrap of shade to another, slinking from the heat. They barely noticed the slight figure waiting for a mango to fall. They chatted, swatted flies and complained about the heat. Gradually they gathered their momentum to go.

Weary old women came on foot, knitted together in twos or threes. Crowded on a long bench by the Chapel entrance, they were waiting to receive one of Frei Timoteo's blessings. They fanned and shaded themselves with pamphlets, swabbed at mizzled brows. Their crumpled faces were icons of enduring faith, cracked as antique lacquer. At long intervals, a heavy wooden door admitted one blessing-seeker. In her hallowed moment with the Frei, each woman felt every ounce of suffering in her life rewarded. And emerged glowing, cleansed by the Frei's wisdom. Drifts of scorched scent escaped each time the door was opened. To Vália it was a torment, though she knew it must be incense.

The sooty smell was from her childhood: smoke was trouble. All those times when police came to the hill in the night. Kids saw them first, from where they flew kites on the rock. No uniforms, but that didn't fool them. You could tell the police anywhere. The kids ran upwards, bursting to tell. But before they got far the first gunshots cracked in the air, rattling tin walls. Reeking fuel emptied around the lower shacks, then a quick getaway, as if it never happened. The first time, Vál)ia couldn't believe it. After that she expected nothing better. She remembered smoky amber glowing on the hillside, panicky voices, running figures. And in the morning, the gloom of wet blackness pervading the remains of homes built only from debris anyway. Steaming stumps and twisted metal. Crouched among the char, black faced and silent, those who had lost a little, which was all that they had.

The baby stirred. She stood to stroll around the compound, bouncing him gently in her arms. Beneath an acacia she stopped for a moment. Joaquim gurgled. She was freckled by the tree's dissected shade, filigree fine after the mango's dense cloak. She tried to resist the impulse to stare at the women and the Frei's door. That smell was in her mouth now, acrid and sooty, lining her tongue with dissolved bitterness.

From the duty box, the guard passed her an irritated look. He spooned rice and beans into his mouth from a foil tin. Under his arms sweat patches spread, leaving maps on his grey, badged shirt. Vál_ia hummed a tune to block out the thought of beans in her stomach. He looked like he could cause trouble with a full belly and nowhere else to spend his energy.

They sat back under their tree, Joaquim restless with the heat. Vál_ia made a game for him with acacia pods. Rattling them, then hiding them behind her back, humming. She smiled with those wide, lively eyes mothers make for babies. He giggled. His flawless face beamed, then grew solemn, seeking the pods and the noise. She let the silence linger, watching his expression. When she shook them for him again, he screamed with delight, and tried to grab a pod.

Out of the museum trailed a small group of schoolchildren clutching merchandise: postcards and posters with images of sin and hellfire, assorted saints, and Christ bleeding for our souls. The kids rolled their eyes, glad to be out, too long under the oppressive gazes of martyrs. Two girls, dragging satchels over the sandy ground, came to sit on a low wall beside Vália's tree. They crouched close together in jeans and grey school tee shirts. Whispering — a crucial debate about a boy, the one loitering near the guard's box. They nudged each other, little high-pitched shrieks and forbidden laughter escaping. Vália used to be the same with Ana, teasing the guys with their clapped out old Vespas, all standing round like they thought they were mechanical geniuses. Outside Ana's dad's bar they would fix each other's hair, dancing around in shorts and high sandals, trading precious secrets and desires. That was until Luiz came along and her belly began to swell the first time.

Now the schoolgirls opened a caramel bar, a drooping tile of sweetness. Fused by the heat to its paper, neither girl had the patience to wrestle for its sticky promise. They cast it onto the wall and went to join their group. Just in time, as the teachers came pacing from the exit.

The mid afternoon sun punished everyone — pores wept, bodies slouched into submission. Vália felt it keenly. Her 'Jesus is Love' shirt clung damply. Such smiling faces, when they gave her that tee shirt at the Universal Church of God is Love. She and Luiz used to go on Wednesday nights. The church was alright until they had to wave money above their heads to show how much they wanted to be saved. Soon all the money Luiz didn't drink would go to Pastor Júlio. And what was left to feed two children with? No wonder her little girl had got sick. Vália began rocking with her son. To and fro, rocking out all her resentment for the past.

A bee came to investigate the caramel, which melted now into the dimples in the stone. It made a curious dance around the sugary pool, nudging with its legs before taking off to circle again. Gingerly, it landed and probed the edge of its caramel lake. Vália stood abruptly, and set off around the compound with Joaquim, too hungry to watch the bee. She couldn't bear to be tempted to scrape up leftovers like that. Her son was getting irritable. Bouncing him impatiently, Vália paced from tree to tree. A jaggedness edged her voice as she tried to quieten the baby.

Pacing couldn't calm either of them. They returned to the bench. The baby was noisy now. Vália slumped heavily against the mango's trunk, unresponsive to Joaquim's wails. Maybe God was deserting her. Maybe she deserved it, tainted as she was with her sooty shadow of guilt. But the babe was an innocent. If she let them find her, he would be left alone in the world. Vália began to curse and cry. Silent tears curling down her nose, hot breathy oaths muttered into her lap. Joaquim, crying louder, drowned out the sound of bad words from his mother's mouth.

She cursed the blessed women by the Frei's door, she cursed the greedy tree, keeping all its fruits, the Frei, too lazy to come out and help people in need, the guard's malign face, and the baby who wouldn't stop crying. Then she cursed God, who turned a deaf ear, and herself, for getting into this mess, sinning, hungry, nowhere to go.

The last cars swung out into the road, with friendly waves and beeps. The guard closed the gate, leaving open

the small pedestrian door. He turned to look for her. Vál
made up her mind, bracing her feet in the dust.

"After six. Time to go, lady." Swinging his keys again.
Vál. sat still, looking straight ahead. "You heard me. Time
to go." Again she stayed still. "No wind, no luck. Try
somewhere else for mangoes." She sat still as the tree.
"*Merda!*" he spat on the ground. He had been expecting
this all day. Should never have let her in. "Move it, you
can't stay here."

Vál. shook her head. "No."

"I warned you this morning. You think this is a shelter
or something?"

She took a deep breath. "I need to see Frei Timoteo."

The guard looked outraged, "You can't! He's busy. You
want to see him, you've got to queue up with the others.
You saw them earlier."

"I have to see him. Tell him a young mother is here with
her baby. Tell him they need help."

"No. Look it's not possible, just move it." This in a lower,
intimidating tone.

"I'm not leaving till I see him." Vál. was nervous but
with the determination of the desperate. "I need him to
confess me."

The guard gave a sigh. He turned away from her and
marched to knock on the heavy wooden door. He rubbed
his forehead agitatedly. As the door opened she could see
him raise his arms and shrug his shoulders in gestures of
helplessness, explaining the nuisance woman. He shook
his head and looked back towards her. A balding head
peered around the door.

She understood everything now. God was angry with
her, that's why he didn't send any wind. She had come

here, the worst type of sinner, to this holy place, expecting shelter and heavenly fruits. What she deserved was to burn in Hell. All she could do now was to confess to Frei Timoteo, throw herself on the mercy of God.

The Frei was crossing the sandy space in grey robes, lit then shaded by sun piercing tree canopies.

Arriving under the mango, he smiled and said, "Good evening, Senhora. The guard tells me you need my help."

Válatia was stuck for words. She looked at her son, quiet again, looking back at his Mama.

"Tell me your name," said Frei Timoteo.

Válatia looked up into his face, lined and wise. His eyes were grey and dappled by the light pattern at the mango's fringe. He was nothing like fat Pastor Júlio.

"Válatia."

"May I sit down, Válatia?"

The Frei sat on the bench leaving space for Válatia to think. He saw Joaquim's petal-eyelids close. Folding his hands in his lap, he waited for Válatia to talk. He was a man who could wait for a long time.

And so she told him the story of homecomings and fear, of unfocused eyes, anger and *cashaça* fumes on the breath. She couldn't stop there; it all came stampeding from her mouth. Out rushed the swaying pauses, sickening anticipation and flesh blenching as punches gained rhythm to become a battering rain. She told of hot tears, of bones that throbbed, and ink-stain blood that spread under the skin. She spoke of heaving snores and darkness coming. More, she mentioned gasoline pouring, precious things bundled and a sleeping child clasped. And now a door closed, a rock or two quietly placed, and a match, flaring, dropped casually as a handkerchief. She finished with the start of a long, hot journey.

Closing her eyes, tears escaping between the lashes, Vál600ia could smell the Eternal Fire sharper than ever. The smoke tainted her own hands, clung in her clothes. Pastor Júlio would have screamed about the Ten Commandments, shame and sin, and the Devil turning us to his own work.

Frei Timoteo told her God could see all her suffering. He sent for the guard to bring a ladder to the tree. In his office of wood, the Frei pressed some coins and a square of paper into her hand. The paper had a name and directions written on.

"It's a quiet place too," he said.

Vál600ia set off across the city, her sleeping babe in arms. She was feeling lighter, despite her sack of mangoes.

We Are All Cut from the Same Cloth

The homesick are a strange tribe — a loose bundle of rags rent from the native cloth, borne around the globe on whimsical currents. Worrying at raw, frayed edges, pulling at the fibres that once laced them to the old place, serves only to slacken and tangle. And then, little by little, as surely as the tide returns, we are stitched into the patchwork of the new place; each hand shaken, each cup of coffee sipped, a tiny, tightening knot.

The Miss Bangú contest was what really stirred things up: all part of Edward's plan to take the mill upmarket. He'd been drafted in to turn things around. Bangú once produced the best cotton in Brazil, but its fortunes flagged and it lost contracts to other big producers. Built in the British style, with red brick chimneys and workers' quarters on site, the mill was a little piece of England's industrial pride transplanted into the heart of Rio de Janeiro. It manufactured bales of sturdy hessian good only for coffee sacks, and a few lines of *chita*, cheap cotton in cheerful prints, beloved of maids and street vendors. Edward refined the process with sophisticated techniques and vowed export-quality cloth would soon roll off Bangú looms.

His innovations had indeed produced a fine cloth. My talents, he outlined evangelically before we left Britain, could bring the factory portfolio bang up-to-date by creating new designs. He never really understood the gulf between botanical painter and textile designer, my being 'artistic' would suffice. I was happy for any excuse to sketch and tempted by the prospect of tropical specimens. Many of the species turned out to be garish to my tastes, artificial-looking, though always an interesting challenge. The word from the loom-foreman, and indeed from Edward, was always to draw less realistically. Exaggerated plant forms were what they wanted: child-like, art-naïf almost. They erased the detail in my drawings, the shading and tendrils, the venation on leaves. The prints they liked best seemed to have no bearing in botanical reality. The colourists who blocked the sketches across the fabric breadth always chose the most clashing inks they could find. I struggled to see any trace of the original sketches in the final fabric. At times I wondered if Edward asked for new designs just to keep me occupied, my work stacking up in a cabinet somewhere without ever reaching the print-setter's desk.

Occasionally he brought me pot-plants from the florist — mainly, I think, to avoid going out of the city. I longed to go to the forest, somewhere green, to sketch and find new specimens. But Edward's life was in the city. Back home, we'd enjoyed strolls on the Downs or in the woods; here in Brazil he was uneasy in natural environments, uncomfortable outside the streets of Laranjeiras, Botafogo and Leme that he loved. In Rio he was so very much at home. His skin took on an oily sheen, as if his pores were breathing more easily. He loosened up his buttons, slackened his tie. He began, in the Brazilian manner, to touch associates on the forearm or the shoulder as they conversed. Bit by bit, his old Britannic ways eased up and he started to give full rein to his urges and appetites. Whereas back home he'd decline a third pint of bitter with a hand waved over the glass, 'Better not: work in the morning,' now he developed a taste for cane-rum and cigars. When not overseeing the looms, he frequented dancing bars and the yacht club. He loved nothing more than to sit on the Beira-Mar watching the girls go by in their colourful beachwear, commenting rapturously on the wonders of the mulatto form.

I, on the other hand, looked and felt every inch the pallid gringo. While my husband sipped coconut *batidas* at the beach bars, observing, learning from the Brazilians at play, I bloomed into a canvas of red, puffed up with mosquito bites and heat rash. Daubed with calamine lotion, I lurked in the shade of enormous hats. Edward made friends and connections. He learned Portuguese quickly. As a well-known local businessman, he was invited to dinners and inaugurations, Chamber of Commerce drinks parties, first nights at the Teatro Nacional. He'd found his niche, become so Brazilian I hardly knew how to behave with him any more.

We were very comfortable by now, compared to our lives in England. A considerable mansion in Botafogo, three mulatto girls as help — all my material needs met; yet comfortable was not how I felt. I was adopted into the circle of ex-pat wives and Brazilian ladies of leisure who kept Rio's coffee houses and boutiques in business. Their rigorous schedule of lunches, charity fundraisers and coffee mornings meant there was theoretically no need to spend a lonely day. The women were kind and they were curious about me. They indicated pastry shops, butchers and beauticians of repute. The Brazilian women had a fatalistic way of talking that the other ex-pats also picked up. Future events were never anticipated without the postscript, '*Se Deus quiser*' — God willing. They spoke of husbands, holidays, the economy, all in the same helpless tone, with ironic shrugs and knowing looks.

"Ricardo has been so foul-tempered lately," said one. "If only he'd find another mistress he might stop pestering me about my Mappin account."

On first hearing these conversations, I felt like an outsider, smug almost, a progressive woman with a career of her own and no understanding of a husband's weakness for mistresses. With the germination of Edward's Miss Bangú idea, growing like a silk grub in its cocoon, I realised with horror that I'd more in common with these women than I thought.

Edward was pleased with his mill. Bangú had shaken off its coffee-sack image. Its delicate, high-grade cotton, soft-on-the-skin, emboldened with exotic motifs, was attractive to the once-elusive European markets.

"*Chita* used to be for the poor," Edward said, "but soon you'll see it on the best-dressed folk — along with British wool, Japanese silk, and French linens."

He intended the fashion houses of Paris and Milan would be cutting this Brazilian cloth within three years, and dreamt up the Miss Bangú contest to promote the mill and its product. The women who worked the looms and printing rollers were each to be given a length of *chita* to make into a dress. The most beautiful design, as modelled by its maker, would win the contest — and the crown of Miss Bangú. The culmination and judging would be based around a pageant. Edward presided over preparations with intense enthusiasm that bordered on lechery. One day I visited his office to find him adjusting seams on a muslin template pinned over the curves of one of the mill girls. He kissed me, received my visit with relaxed good humour, as if this was all in a day's work: his fingers moving over the girl's skin, separated from her only by the filmy warp and weft of muslin. From that moment on, my waking moments were focused on one terrible possibility — Edward betraying me with an affair. I panicked, fretted about ways to stop it. Tactic number one was to invigilate his life, clinging on his arm at every social function, events I normally avoided. But this was doomed. Of course he would behave when I was there. I would not uncover or prevent anything that way. If he was determined, it would only make him devious. My thoughts turned then to how I'd cope if infidelity was, as seemed inevitable, to happen. I practiced nonchalant retorts and brave smiles, planned confident outfits, a united public front.

That spring, the newspapers were lurid with a Parliamentary corruption scandal. An opposition party spokesman triumphed with a line that became famous, "This, Senador, is like lipstick on the collar: it is inexplicable."

My husband's collar had lipstick on it, and it was not the pale coral I was accustomed to wearing.

As the furore built towards the contest, Edward spent every minute at the mill. My despair deepened. I landed on the idea of talking to the maid, a tactic copied from one of the ex-pat women. Eleanora was plumping pillows in the top bedroom. Getting to the point took me a while — it was humiliating. I spoke of Edward being under pressure, and perhaps a little out of sorts, eventually, circuitously concluding, would she let me know if she noticed anything "untoward". Eleanora fiddled with her crucifix necklace as I spoke. She looked at her feet. It took me far too long to realise, as my eyes lifted from her cheap sandals to her blushing cheeks: the maid herself was something "untoward".

Numb, I sat on the bed. The maid left silently. I wondered where to look next. Olga the cook was old, but even she had started wearing her hair a little fancier lately. My mind filled with hellish scenes of lust, sweating bodies, Edward entangled in the limbs of almost every female I had met since arriving.

"He couldn't." I shivered, but a long strand of self-pity had unravelled itself. I don't know how long I sat there trying to reel it in again. Bilious, lost in time, I perched on the freshly changed bed, a statue in a snowdrift. Later, I heard the whirring of the sewing machine. Eleanora was working on new sitting-room drapes.

And that was the noise that cut through my thoughts, an industrious sound luring me downstairs. Eleanora gave me that strange wary look of hers, turning from the machine, sweat spangling her hairline. She'd been through every incarnation in my mind — ally, suspect, rival, whore. Yet the girl before me now was just sweet, hard-working Eleanora. She edged over to make room, barely stopping her foot on the pedal. The needle stamped up and down on the needle-plate in a fury. The maid's deft fingers fed raw-edged damask to the machine's stammering mouth. It ran out neatly hemmed on the other side. She sat straight-backed, her eyes creeping to the left now and then, seeking some sign of what I wanted. She cut thread and knotted one end, light glancing off her red-lacquered nails. She wetted the other end to a point by drawing it through her plump lips.

"Show me," I said.

She turned and looked at me.

"Show me how."

And of course, she obliged. By Eleanora's side, I learned to cut and seam fabric pieces together, to make stitches longer when stitching curves. From a deep blue *chita* sprigged with red, we made a bodice and full dirndl, plumped with calico underskirts. For the first time, I thought I recognised my original sketch of Monkey Grape in the fabric. When she understood my plan more fully, she became a dedicated accomplice. The lessons ranged beyond dressmaking. She taught me homespun beauty-salon tricks and without knowing it, the Brazilian knack of finding sensual pleasure in humble things: sweet mangoes, clean laundry, a cheap lipstick. She painted my nails, pinned my hair up. She powdered my face and slicked black lines along my eyelids. Up close I could smell her warm skin, Leite de Rosas cologne and the faint sweat worked up during her household duties. When she'd finished, I almost looked like I belonged here. Eleanora's hand-stitching was far neater than mine. Some of the hems on the gown were more her work than mine. That, I suppose, may technically have been against the rules.

Poor Edward, I don't believe he was thinking much about rules when I flounced onto the Miss Bangú catwalk in my gown of *chita*. His cigar dropped to the floor, his jaw hung open. Something changed that night — something more than my wearing bright mill-cloth for the first time. I can't fathom it exactly, but, when he beams at me across the dinner table, asking 'More wine, *meu amor?*' I can only think it was the *chita*, bringing out the colour of my eyes.

The Girl in the Song

I hold my breath, like always, as Salvador raises his arm. Muscles move, rope-like, under brown skin. The coconut teeters on the bar edge, pea-green, beaded with cold. Sscchoum! His machete bites to its white heart — and again — before I can breathe out. No fingers lost; they're sure, experienced fingers, curled around the nut snugly, sinking straws into the pale well. Sitting facing the ocean, I sip the salt-sweet coconut-water, just another body among the dog walkers and roller-bladers.

"Bliss! It's so tense at home."

A song drizzles from the radio. Of all the songs that could have played at that moment, it had to be this. Salvador winks at me, over his clinking bottles. I shrug.

"Oh come on, Lo, you were all those things: golden, lovely — still are. Don't you remember the furore you caused back then?" He wipes the machete blade. "The buzz of the city? This tune brings it all back every time."

January's hot breath scours my face, and sun slices everything into black shade and blinding bright. I smile. A tight little lip-stretch.

"Ah, sorry, *minha flor*. You'd rather forget all that now, eh?" He nods stiffly, turns to tidy his liquor bottles.

"It's not you," I tell him, "just those lawyers again and the journalists after their pound of flesh. This time I'm trying to ignore it all."

Mirrored hotels along Avenida Atlantica hug the elegant sweep of Ipanema beach, nudging powdery sand towards the ocean.

He smiles, comes out of his kiosk. "Those were great days, though. Everyone who was anybody came to visit Rio, eh girl?" He's polishing a glass in a cloth.

"Yeah, Bardot, Sinatra..."

"There was something special about then, and our Bossa Nova. Who imagined how far one little tune would go? The world decided it had to be That Song." Salvador's eyes cloud over, agates netted in brown lines. Beyond him the ocean sparkles green. "Funny, the fuss over our little beach, eh?"

We look back, to where the cafe used to be, across the Avenida, now the Caesar Palace Hotel.

"Bet Vinícius couldn't believe his luck. One day just another hopeful, scribbling poetry on napkins, the next his lyrics springing out of radios, tip-starved waiters suddenly desperate to bring his next *cafezinho*. And what about The Girl?"

I'm smiling now, biting the straw flat. "The Girl from Ipanema was poor as a church mouse. Too busy having fun on the beach." We laugh, and for a moment I forget. "How did it all turn so ugly, Salvador?" draining my coconut. "*Aiee!* All those fake blondes doing TV interviews."

He winces. "Fake cheekbones, fake chests, lying through their teeth. Even after Vinícius published the true identity in that magazine. So shameless, Lo."

With the heels of my hands, I hitch my temples up, like a bad face-lift. "So how do you stay looking good, Ms Ipanema?" It's my phoniest TV voice. "Ooooh, I work out a lot — I mean *a lot*, on Ipanema beach, of course. I try to stay just like I was in the song."

Salvador covers his eyes, chuckling.

We look out to sea for a while. On Saturdays the beach is packed. Men peddling skewered shrimp inch, barefoot, among toasting bodies and volleyball squads.

"It's the in-laws that are most upsetting, though, Salvador. That song was famous before they came along. It made enough money for everyone, but now they call The Girl, the very inspiration, a 'gold digger'."

"That's fame and money, *querida*, make you greedy."

"I suppose."

"Vinícius, though, he didn't change. Loved his muse, eh? Jotted down his feelings for her after too many *cafezinhos*, and they made him famous. But, that's how he lived, rich or poor, girls and liquor. Died that way too. Tom was wiser. Scrawled his melodies and invested well. Now even the airport's named after him."

"Maybe the in-laws got tired of hearing about Her, always 'young and lovely'. Money wasn't enough. Could be the real reason they're in court. Put the Golden Girl in her place."

"Yep. Envy, Lo. Nothing to do with 'exploiting the work of a great composer'."

"Vinícius wrote so sweetly. Now certain people have only bitter things to say. *'That woman is a cheap profiteer, Your Honour.'* And carping to the newspapers, *'She doesn't deserve one centavo.'* I bet he and Tom are turning in their graves."

A girl with a shy grin moves along the wave-tiled promenade towards me, in her wrap and pink bikini.

Her hips move in a languorous wave, not so much a samba — only a poet could describe it like that, only Vinícius — but something freer, more natural, unconstrained by the bars of a composer's pen. She moves like the play of a breeze in the palms, with all the exuberance that's her right as a young woman. And the world really does seem to fill with grace — and to smile — as she passes.

Salvador whistles. The girl laughs and runs to kiss me, wooden sandals clattering.

"Try a coconut water, they're sweet today."

Salvador chops another one, as I — I can't help it — the fear of that blade slipping never leaves me — turn my head away. We're roasting like shrimps, Leila is pink along her nose and cheeks. She presses the icy coconut on her belly, sits to tell me about her day. A boy comes to deliver Salvador's newspaper. He leans his bony elbows on the kiosk for a long time, glancing towards Leila when he thinks no one sees.

There's a muffled shout from the kiosk. Salvador's chewing roasted corncob and can barely speak for kernels in his teeth. He's stubbing his finger rhythmically on a page of *O Globo* spread on the counter. There we are in black and white, an old photo of Leila and me smiling, Ipanema beach sweeping away in the background. My stomach clenches: the court verdict.

"SUN SHINES ON THE GIRL FROM IPANEMA". I don't register the headline, don't trust its jolly tone until I've read the important words. 'Judge Mendes ruled in favour of Helô 'Lolo' Martolio, immortalised in the famous song. She will continue to have the right to use the name 'Girl from Ipanema', for her clothing shop. The composer's representatives reacted...'

But that's enough.

Leila, slurping her coconut noisily as she reads along, squeals, throwing her arms around my neck, "*Aaiiee, Mamãe*, we won, we won!"

Salvador kisses us both. "Bravo, my Girls from Ipanema."

He says we deserved it, and how could the Judge go against us? It's just like old times, he laughs, when I used to come with a few *cruzeiros* for a coconut and smile shyly at him. Except now he has two *Garotas de Ipanema*. He starts to sing the song all over, the old charmer, turning to each of us, his agate eyes tender with the lyrics. He has all the moves of a star crooner performing his signature number, just one more time. We dance a giggly samba, and Salvador breaks open some beers. Leila's mobile beeps. Célia. The shop phone's going mad — newspapers after quotes. She passes the phone. I look at Leila — can't they guess we'd be here on the beach?

"The Girls from Ipanema are a bit busy, Célia. Tell them no comment."

THE CELESTINE RECIPE

'A Cake to Please Mothers-in-Law' was created while newly-wed Senhora Souza awaited her first visit from Dona Magrella IV. Benita, the Souza family cook, invented the recipe while her mistress, the novice lady-of-the-house, paced the hallway, weak with nerves. Her imminent guest was known as much for her diminutive frame as the enormous ill-temper it housed.

Benita the cook, uneasy with domestic tensions, scanned her pantry for remedies. A lazy fly, alighting on a scuttle of sweet potatoes, drew her attention to their skin: smooth mauve tattooed by dusty light coming through the ventilation bricks. Thirty minutes later, the stove was wheezing warm sweetness through the house. When beaky little Dona Magrella stabbed her fingers at the cake-stand for a slice of the new recipe, she was suspicious of its plummy hue. Her daughter-in-law, collarbones peppered in nervous rashes, dug her nails into her palm, unable to watch. The effect was almost narcotic. Golden-pink morsels of honeyed potato-and-cornmeal melted on the sharpest tongue in Bom Jesus district, hints of warm nutmeg and cream perhaps stirring some memory of goodness in the old crow. It was some time before she spoke again. When she did, it was to compliment her daughter-in-law's delicate lacework collar.

Senhor Fradique Souza's formidable girth was already testament to Benita's culinary skill. But taming his mother, the fearsome Magrella, brought the Souza family cook new status as a culinary alchemist, with Senhora Souza her most ardent fan. Next day, the lady-of-the-house accompanied her conjurer-cook to the provisions store, Benita for the first time travelling in the comfort of the sulky. Senhor Joaquim, the grocer, restrained his urge to indulge in gossip. The lady opened a special account so that her cook could have whatever she needed. Benita's suggestions for ingredients never more met with refusal. Later, the Senhora insisted on recording the miraculous 'Cake to Please Mothers-in-Law' recipe with laboured scratchings of her ink pen. This same ritual would follow whenever a new dish was concocted. Benita, flushed and floury, struggled to recall every smidgen added while the Senhora scribed. The cook couldn't read the recipes, but her mistress, never again afraid of her mother-in-law, understood their power.

Mostly, Benita relied on her repertoire of traditional Brazilian recipes. No one complained. But the remarkable dishes recorded in the household archive were invented at times of crisis or celebration, generally named after the event to which they owed their genesis. So there was 'Butter-Baked Baptismal Bread', marking baby Fradique Junior's christening, and 'Imperial Biscuits', when Dom Pedro II acceded the throne. The restorative 'Cake to Comfort Storm Survivors', was baked for Senhor Souza and his men following a valiant and muddy battle to save coffee terraces collapsing in a rainstorm. Over time, the Souza family recipe book filled up, and Benita's reputation spread.

That same rainy season of the coffee-terrace mudslide, Benita encountered an unfamiliar woman ordering supplies at Joaquim's grocery. The stranger departed tall and stiff, dressed in a curious mix of humble ticking covering skirts of rich brocade, just glimpsed around the hems, in parlous states of tattering.

Grocer Joaquim was unable to oblige further details of his new customer. Senhor Zé Lima however, stopping to buy sugar for his corner café, had watched the old black woman arrive the day before, bearing cloth bundles on a pole and two cantankerous guinea fowl. She apparently settled herself down by the riverbank. He'd heard sounds of knocking and woodcutting ever since. Benita returned to the Fazenda Fortuna, her day enlivened with a little gossip, to uncover the morning's well-risen dough.

Later in the week, returning to the store, Benita noticed a huddle in the square. The bodies obscured the object of their attention. Curiosity drew her closer. Someone sat on a crate at the crowd's centre, the same strange black woman she'd noticed last time. Benita felt something close to effrontery that the townsfolk should pay so much attention to the eccentrically dressed new arrival. When a mother emerged from the huddle, her children in high spirits, Benita saw with a jolt that they clutched sticky-pumpkin cupcakes. The incomer was selling sweetmeats, bold as you like!

Over the following weeks, Benita's enquiries revealed that Bom Jesus' new confectioner was known as Dona Celestina. Despite countless theories, her origins were undetermined: most likely she'd been indentured as a slave on one of the big plantations, and somehow, legally or otherwise, won her emancipation. That was the detail that least interested Benita. What aggrieved her was the challenge to her status. Bom Jesus had never before had a street-vendor of confectionery. The estates had their own cooks to provide meals and sweetmeats for staff and family. Some even had their secret recipes, though none with the hallowed potency of Benita's coveted formulae. The 'Cake to Please Mothers-in-Law', now legendary, inspired hushed reverence among the region's kitchen workers. Benita consoled herself, kneading dough rhythmically, with the notion that the new Confection'ress was drawing crowds with her novelty value. It could not last.

Senhora Souza was expecting a second child. Fradique Junior was now consuming Benita's vegetable purees with gusto, and testing the patience of his governess. The expectant mother confided to Benita her certainty that this one would be a girl. To celebrate the birth, a special dish would be required. Benita got to work imagining the flavours most befitting the blessing of baby girls. There would be sugared roses and ground almonds, for sure. For a while she forgot her rival, reassured of her place at the heart of the Souza family farm.

Quite pale with morning sickness, the Senhora sent to the kitchen several times a day for fennel tea. That this confinement should be so unlike the last, only strengthened her belief that she was carrying a girl. Benita cooked eggs to fortify her, but they were returned uneaten. Senhor Fradique looked a little helpless, alone at the breakfast table. The new recipe would be rich and sweet, incorporating all the things the poor Senhora loved, but had to forfeit until her term was complete. Benita made experimental batches whenever time allowed.

A kitchen maid, sent off to buy butter, was asked to bring extra for these experimentations. Returning from her errand, she poked her head into the kitchen then disappeared, forgetting to leave the butter on the table. Benita went to find her. The girl shrieked as the cook disturbed her in the laundry. The pies the young maid had been hiding fell spinning to the floor. When they came to rest, Benita froze: four of Dona Celestina's Sticky-Pumpkin Cupcakes, brazenly dishevelled.

The kitchen girl wrung her hands. "They for the Senhora. She terrible cravin' for them."

Celestina, relegated to the periphery of Benita's thoughts lately, now returned triumphant and taunting. The cook wondered how many others in the household were slyly nibbling that woman's confections, keeping stashes around the farm. These maudlin thoughts fuelled her rhythm, working gammon steaks with a tenderiser, her forehead pinching into a deep scribble. The bell rang, summoning more fennel tea that the kitchen maid scurried to pour from the kettle. As her footsteps faded on the staircase, Benita felt a punch of betrayal and wondered if her glory days were over.

Headed for town next day, Benita saw her rival laden with sacks of meal, trudging homewards. Dona Celestina nodded politely. The Souza family cook looked pointedly away. There followed a catalogue of similar slights. Celestina was bumped in the doorway of the store in a manner that could almost have been accidental. Her greetings were ignored, and sudden, echoing silence descended when she entered the store to find Benita conversing with the proprietor. Celestina never showed vexation at this sorry treatment. Much to the chagrin of Fortuna Farm cook, the confectioner, apparently used to hostility, behaved with perfect civility.

Benita, battling to reconcile her poor manners with her true nature, which she felt to be neither mean nor rude, justified this bullying campaign as a survival tactic. Sustained hostility (her rashly-conceived strategy to drive away the threat) was not in her nature, but this was a war of reputation and favour, one that could not be won by befriending the enemy.

The sky was bruised and sulphurous, a filthy rain lashing roof-tiles loose, when Senhora Souza began her labour. Three hissing kettles were attended by a flurry of maids shuttling to her room with compresses, and back to stir up the fire in the range. Like the nine months preceding, the birth was complicated. Tortured screams rent the very plaster of the walls, and the kitchen girls were white with horror. In the small hours, a tiny voice was heard, but many more hours passed before the doctor descended. The Senhora, he said, had lost a great deal of blood, and must stay abed. Benita must prepare wholesome broths to strengthen her. He rolled his hat in his hands, eyes pale with weariness, and left in the dwindling rain.

Baby Hortensia was skinny and unnaturally quiet. Fradique Junior was a little wary of his mother, so limp and still. Benita boiled lamb shanks, chopped potatoes and collards, and served the broth with warm milk loaves — invalid food to tempt the Senhora. When she went to town for provisioning, tight bunches of folks still crowded Celestina's stall, and she cursed the woman to highest heaven. When her mistress recovered, she would cook her very best recipes, adding little extras here and there. The smells from the kitchen would be so good, the Souza household would forget all about Celestina's sugary fare.

After fifteen days, Senhora Souza rose to sit by the window, a little pinker in the cheeks.

To Benita, she said, "I haven't forgotten our agreement. Hortensia is a hard-won blessing, a reason to celebrate."

So a date was set, and the cook began in earnest to create 'Hortensia's Cake'.

The recipe was meticulously itemised in Benita's head: cane sugar, sweet almonds, fresh eggs, pounds of wheat- and corn flour, rosewater, orange rind, leavening and treacly lumps of Muscovado. Kitchen maids were enlisted to sift flour and frost rosebuds. Benita kept for herself the exacting task of measuring rosewater and grated rind.

Whisking egg whites to peaks would be done at the last minute, to keep the air in. "Now...." She surveyed the ranks of ingredients, small pearls of sweat massing on her cheeks. "Oh, Lord have mercy."

The kitchen girls stared.

"The almonds. I clean forgot them." She departed in a panic for the store, reciting her recipe for fear of other omissions. Her heart raced and the sun gnawed at her neck.

Limping into Joaquim's store, she gripped the counter, exclaiming, "Oh, Senhor, you are the gladdest sight, I swear it."

The grocer smiled cautiously.

Benita wheezed, "Sell me a quart of almonds, and you'll be saving a life. *Aiiee*, what a heat." She closed her eyes for a moment, her hair escaping its pins in places.

"I'm afraid I won't be your saviour today, Senhora. The harvest was poor. Half went spoiling in those unseasonable rains."

Benita flushed and gulped, apparently experiencing some form of respiratory difficulty. Her mouth flapped like a bated pike, and she stared at the grocer, her old friend, as if she did not recognise his face.

"But...it...it's most urgent..." She stopped and bit her lip.

The grocer looked around at his shelves. "It's just possible..."

Benita's eyes searched his face.

"Good Dona Celestina bought the last almonds a few weeks back. She might be your saviour."

The cook's expression as she backed out of the shop left the grocer frowning, no wiser as to whether he'd helped or hindered the situation.

Benita shuffled beneath dripping banana leaves. Guinea fowl began a high-pitched yammering and the track opened onto a riverbank hut flanked by cashew trees. Behind, the river Paraíba flowed, molten gold between low boughs. Wood-smoke and toffee scented the air.

"Ah-hum...good day to you." Benita's voice was small.

Dona Celestina, stoking a brick oven, looked up.

"You must think me unforgivable... I... it's... there is an important occasion, and without almonds..." Benita stammered. "Senhor Jo said..."

Shooing the guinea fowl, the arch-rival was gone inside her hut, reappearing with a paper packet. Pressed into Benita's hands, the copper-skinned nuts filled her nostrils with sweet spice as she fumbled for her purse.

Celestina frowned sternly. She wouldn't take payment.

At Fazenda Fortuna the kitchen is glad with sunlight, the stove is fierce. Hortensia, angelic on her mother's lap, is swathed in crochet. Padre Melo sips coffee on the terrace with the family while Benita steals unnoticed through the back courtyard. Dona Celestina's almonds are pulverised under impatient hands. The feral pounding drives the Padre away to pace in the orchard. Benita's deft whisk coaxes egg whites into snowscapes. The delicate scents that emerge more than compensate for the violence and din.

Everyone agrees, as the sun slides low, that 'Hortensia's Cake' is sublime. The grainy intensity of almonds silences the gathering, the subtlety of roses and muscovado's dark sweetness bring smiles and comfort. Senhor and Senhora Souza clasp hands, Hortensia gurgles contentedly, and Benita, clearing away the empty cake stand, sighs happily.

As they recall the recipe for the archive that evening, Senhora Souza remarks, "Sometimes I think you are not a cook, Benita, but some kind of sorceress."

Celestina is singing, packing up puddings for her stall, as Benita arrives next morning. Silently, Benita holds out a box for her old rival. The Confection'ress of Bom Jesus comes to face her. Benita nods, urging the parcel forwards. Inside a crumple of wax paper, lies a still-warm cake releasing sweet scents. Benita hands Celestina an envelope. Unable to read the contents herself, and unsure whether Celestina can, she tells her more or less what Senhora Souza has written. It's the new recipe for this 'Cake for Friendship': warming ginger, sweet honey to counter bitterness, and the fat promise of the plumpest papaya on the Fortuna Farm.

Vodka on the Rocks

Seduction's the art I was born to. What else do you do with cascading locks that fan like goose-down in the open sea? These come-with-me eyes never fail; emerald marbles fished from the seabed. Glassy waves lick light over my pale curves and scales - a portrait in silver, reflecting fishermen's solitude. They're helpless these poor delirious sailor-boys far from home. My voice is a dangerous lullaby.

They're not so gullible now as in the old days. Back then — just a wooden hull keeping them from the sea and all her fury — they believed in anything. 'Course they had a few tricks to quell the terror, a Lubber's Lanyard held the rigging here, a Ringbolt Hitch there, but really, they were no protection from the hunger of the waves. Once they'd landed in a dark harbour, it was all hard liquor and lurid yarns, the soft pillow of a girl's shoulder. Then back to the livid blue swell. That twilight life! No wonder they fell for myths. Half set sail without so much as a whisker sprouted on their apple-cheeks. Crazed with hunger and scurvy, hallucinating score-legged serpents, they clung to signs and charms, any shred of hope for mercy on a cruel sea. My little chorus was quite a relief, I expect, soothing, like angels watching over them, perhaps. Hark at me getting fanciful! But it was easier then, minnows to the bait, they were.

So much for seduction. It's getting them to stay that's the tricky bit — 'least that's where I fall down. My strongest wish is to keep them with me, to have a Mer-Prince to flip his fins and dive deep with me. Somehow, however hard I try to pass on my silvered lungs and swimming muscles, their earthly flesh fails to cross into my watery world. Oh, the desperate hours I've spent, among corals and waving weed, as another handsome one turns cold on my chest. Oh, the shame when they float away, and the shrimps start their vile feast. Where does it go wrong?

The art of luring is not what it was. Some of the old girls have given up on this lonely game, tired of the company of seals. I've seen grand dames, barnacled round the gills, all silted up. They creep to the bottom, get crusted about with bones and coins, and lurk like hermit crabs. What a way to go. Well it's not going to be me. I'm no quitter. I run through my arpeggios in a cave with good acoustics — keep the old voice oiled. This hair is a lot of work too. Not all glamour, see? Even for high-maintenance sirens, the seduction business is tough these days.

Technology is what we're up against. Look at them, so smug now with their satellite-positioning systems and their radar. Hulks of bullish metal, bruising through the deep — like nothing would stop them. At those speeds, there's no time for romancing. Liners, I don't give a second glance. I hold out for the older models — cargo boats, trundling in from other decades. They're the poor relations, I suppose, but a girl has to take her chance when it comes.

There's one on its way now, a Russian freighter, creaking and slow. They've been many a month at sea, eking out their rye bread through Arctic steam and the endless Atlantic, to the flotsam of the Tropics. Two men were lost in a storm up north; no one spoke of it, each sailor tending his own mute hatred of the waves. Last contact with their women folk was eight months ago, poor souls. Rations are running as low as crew morale. Their horn is a howl, piercing the engine's weary grind, their pale faces, expressionless, fix on the horizon.

And here sit I on my rock among the algae. It's a balmy night, a warm tropical rain falling, my favourite weather. Soft drops pucker the surface and lose themselves. The rain blurs my eyes and everything is rinsed and renewed. My voice is pure like I never heard it before and I think surely it's getting better with age. The Russians don't know of the skeletons of iron, swollen with rust, languishing hereabouts. Nor of horizontal, sleeping masts, nor ruptured hulls with curious fish threading through, china cups seeded among the coral. I imagine for a second, the warm surety of a Mer-man by my side, reflecting my smiles and my heart pounds so that it almost hurts. I lift my voice in chorus with the waves and the rain's sweet percussion, singing my heart out for the love of a sailor.

The raindrops reverberate, passing music over waves, lulling icy Russian ears. I am their pole, stronger than any compass bearing. First though, there are the rocks. Calmly, almost, the listing grey bulk descends, cold metal sucked down by the ravenous sea. The crew face their fate nobly, with relief even, their shouts muffled by rain clouds.

Here he is, my Russian water-boy, struggling no more. Arcing underneath his falling form, I bear him upwards again, so many warm pulses weighing in my arms. He is clean-shaven and blond, peaceful-looking. We breach the surface, The Murmansk already nudging the sandy bottom, another secret skeleton. He splutters, opens his eyes and stares into my salt-washed emeralds. Pale irises contract, like gravel stirred by tides, but whether it's fear or rapture, I cannot tell. I kiss him, his mouth tastes sweet as rain on my salted lips, then pull down and down. Finning frantically, churning like a whirlpool, I think I might burst with the effort. All the while I exhale damp, amphibian breath into him, chasing air from his pink lungs. His teeth are smooth as pearls; nervous bumps on his chest press into mine.

Only now, wheezing among weedy relics, do I notice the rainbow glimmer over his thighs. Looking again, I laugh and laugh. He's grinning shyly, all Mer-man, flexing a fine silver-green tail gilded with violet iridescence. Most wonderful of all, as I float up closer, are those little pulsings of his ribs. He can stay, washing about my salty domain with me! Which of us is the more shocked, I couldn't say.

Was I ever happier? Together we visit every marvel and curiosity of the seabed, sculpted rooms of coral he never imagined existed, sea caves sheltering spangled eels, and glowing curtains of wrack like forgotten theatre backdrops. We swim through all the shades of the sea, forgetting the loneliness that had haunted us once. He wants to know the ocean-lore, to hear those sailors' yarns from the other side of the mirror. I tell him all I know, of wise old turtles and the fellow who inhabited a whale's stomach, my versions of Atlantis, Marie Rose, Endeavour and the Titanic. Still he's eager for more: sea sprites; man-saving dolphins; and a fevered Mr Wallace, shipless, whose creatures in jars, decades in classification, jumbled on the Caribbean swell. I shed fifty years and everything glows.

One thing bothers me. Why didn't I notice it sooner? It's like a closed place deep in his eyes, a flatness that does not reflect my smile. He's sweet and kind, and enchanted by me. His little gestures, like magic remedies, erase my old days of loneliness. But it remains, a tiny pebble at the back of his gaze.

Now I've seen it, it's like an unscratchable itch. Each time we sigh into each other's eyes, it greets me. In such a short time, the terrible dark thing in his look has infected us.

There, between his brows, a deep crease appears. He mentions my tail is getting ragged. He's gazing into vaulted coral chambers, where svelte young mer-maidens fan their perfect tails. He no longer nudges fat crayfish into my mouth, peppered with kisses, but pointedly announces he's hungry. He waits, then, while I hunt his food. In a panic, I tell the Scandinavian tale of the Little Mer-girl. He looks bored. Do I have to talk so much?

Happiness washes away like driftwood. I become a mute fish by his side, not bothering to comment on the painted crabs we see.

Our bleak meanderings take us back to the wreck of the Murmansk. He goes off to explore the rusting nooks and remnants of his sailor days. I wait, numb, among the scattered cargo of vodka crates. Finning back to me his look has a terrible cast, screening him off like fishing nets, his gravely irises blinkered with scales. So it becomes clear. The stony core that resents me belongs with them, the Russian folk, his girl, the nights of drinking and song that keep out the cold.

We erupt at the surface. A far-off rumbling had announced a vessel approaching. Quickly, I put my mouth to his, breathe out lungfuls of remorse and feel his borrowed amphibian air slink back to me, a bitter last kiss. He gasps, the salt stinging at his throat, hot with blood once more. He looks at me with strange gratitude and turns to wave at the oncoming ship. Cold waves push between us, rhythmically stretching out my sadness.

Back, then, to starlit cantatas here on my rock. The seals are out tonight, tumbling at the surface, carefree. They swivel their heads in my direction, sensing something new in my voice, "La. La-ah, la-ah, la-ah, la, la, la."
There's a different lilt to my song, I suppose, a gentler rhythm, perhaps a hopeful note or two. An old girl like me can still adapt, and maybe I can shed these jealous little scales. They're just one or two, but then it only takes a trickle of oil to blacken a mile of ocean. The seals swim closer now, nosing me with curious, twitching whiskers, and for a moment I envy their simple lives, split between wave and shore, with instinct to guide them always, funny old things. A rickety Nicaraguan cruiser breaches the horizon, bound for Guanabara Bay. The full moon gilds my scales, and the clear air carries my song far. My time to settle on the bottom, growing barnacles, is a long way off.

Northern Species

"The best way, see, is to go with their routine. Roost with them; wait 'til they bed down. Quiet as a spider, let your nets down over the nesting holes. Then just wait. Drink coffee, count the stars." A toothpick dances between Senhor Mendes' marooned front teeth. "At daybreak, they gotta get food, right? Pronto, into your net. Then, jus' like fishing, haul 'em in. It's a lotta noise, but look around this place, who's gonna hear?"

Dawn is coming, dampening the ground. Senhor Joaquim Mendes feels his bones stiff. Mauro's clothes are crumpled and gritty. The men peer down into the canyon. Opposite, a blue macaw scuffles from a nest-hole in glowing sandstone, and flies east towards the light. Other birds begin to stir, and something twitches Mauro and Joaquim Mendes' net.

"Now!"

Uncle and nephew work the net. They have a bird. It screeches murderously. The noise, bowling along the canyon, spreads panic among the emerging roost. Claws tangle, feathers poke through the nylon webbing.

Mauro is surprised by the strength of it. "Shut up," he implores. "Son of a bitch."

Tense with the effort not to snag the swaying load on outcrops, they finally land it at their feet. Breathing hard, admiring its hyacinth plumage, they unhook each tiny knot from the scratching claws. Struggling, gnashing its thick beak, the bird is unable to resist four hands cramming it inside a crate, strapping the crate to a bicycle. Joaquim straddles the bike, his broad foot pawing for the pedals. Hurling an empty *cashaça* bottle into the canyon, Mauro perches behind, twisting awkwardly to secure the cargo.

A distant 'chink' echoes as the bottle hits the canyon-floor and the flock's uproar recedes. Mauro and his uncle Joaquim creak and wobble along red powder roads in the creeping light. The bird rebels, batting against its confines.

"How much will it fetch, Tio?" Mauro's voice ululates as they bounce over ruts.

"Few thousand at least — they're rare now. Paired up with that other Pretty Polly back at your place, much more."

In the distance, a low-grinding engine toils.

"Tractor," assures Uncle Joaquim over his shoulder. "Only farmers here 'bouts."

Mauro keeps his cool, trying to ignore the sound. "Who the hell buys these screechers? Rich gringos?"

"Eventually. Europeans or Americanos with more money than sense."

The engine gets louder. A Toyota jeep turns into the track, twenty yards ahead. The driver, wearing a shirt with epaulettes, leans out.

"*Merda.*" Uncle Joaquim stops pedalling.

"*Hein, hein,* gentlemen, what you got there?" The door panel reads 'POLICIA FLORESTAL'.

Joaquim smiles hastily, his wizened stubble creasing. "Just a lame birdie. We... uh... lookin' after 'im."

The officer jumps down, takes the crate from Mauro's grasp. The macaw screeches. The nets, rolled underneath, spring loose.

"You come out at dawn — with nets — to help lame birds?" His lip curls.

Joaquim Mendes' bicycle tracks end right there. Lone Toyota tracks continue on the red road towards town, Mauro and his uncle handcuffed in the rear partition, the hopeful light gone from their eyes. The bird rides in the passenger seat, crooning softly as the sky takes on the colour of ripe corn.

And so the two of them got banged up. Hapless Uncle Joaquim was always in some sort of trouble, but Mauro? Ferociously, she swept dust out of the front door, her thoughts tumbling fast behind the broom. She'd never realised he was such a dumb ass. Had he forgotten the police raids on TV? The fool. He'd tried to pacify her about the first macaw with talk of some trucker mate who'd take it to Rio airport, the money that would solve all their debt worries. Just one more trip to get a partner bird, he said, and they'd be laughing. A fool's dream, like all the schemes of destitute Northern farmers. She lay awake nights wondering what to do with five acres of barren red dust and a small baby. She had hidden the first bird — the one they'd got away with — in the cassava-root store, for fear of the police coming searching. The blessed creature shredded the newspaper lining its cage for three days solid, making a nest, clucking like a hen. She heard Mauro had since been bailed. Well if he had, he never came for her.

From the porch, her jaded eye contemplated drought-whipped acres and broken trees, wondering how life would be if she'd been born in the south, or east. Brazil overflowed with natural riches: Amazonia, awash with rain, gold, mahogany; the South East, fat on beef-pasture and coffee estates, soap opera people flouncing around glossy air-conditioned malls. But she belonged to the forgotten

Northeast, among ossified farmers watching the sky in vain hope. A small child laboured on the ochre expanse of her neighbour's fields, skinning shrivelled roots with a knife too big for his hands. Sun roasted his back, hot wind glazed his skin and hair with red dust, like a terracotta relic ploughed up after centuries buried. They showed scenes like this whenever the 'Nordeste' was on TV news; people in the South must watch tutting and shaking their heads. She vowed her son would not grow up like that, a desiccated little workhorse of sun-baked clay. He'd play in the shade of broad trees, walk to school in gentle rain. All the money Mauro talked of would have got them out — to some place milder, where the sky shed tears of pity on the earth now and then.

Her ears were drawn to strange cawing from the outbuildings. The macaw sat blinking among newspaper curls, breast feathers parting to reveal a chalky egg. She stared at it, a pearl nestled in blue velvet. One hundred thousand *reais*, Mauro had bragged, for a pair.

They made a wretched couple, she struggling alone to care for the boy and no rain on the fields for another year, the macaw with only its egg for company in the root-house. Surrounding them, broken-stemmed cassava withered in drunken rows, witness to the sky's spiteful heart. The trucker who was to carry the bird-cargo south never called. Maybe news of Mauro's capture had reached him.

And so she went to town, her son strapped to her back, her head held high as curious neighbours peered in her direction. At the mill-yard, no sign of the broad man who once had helped Mauro bring home a plough-horse. Men loading flour sacks avoided her eyes. They muttered something about a bakery gesturing towards the rusting gate, then turned their powdery backs. The trucker watched her approach, munching buttered bread, his coffee steaming on the counter. He dusted his hand before shaking hers. She asked him would he come to the house.

Driving back across her five sorry acres, the truck's bouncing rhythm over potholes sent her boy to sleep. She headed across the yard to brew fresh coffee, directing the trucker towards the root-house. Half way to the house she froze: unfamiliar car-tracks printed the dust, and her front door stood ajar. She shivered, hugging her son to her. Her first thought was Mauro. Saucepans and crockery were scattered, chairs upended. From the outbuildings, the trucker yelled. The cage was empty — the bird gone. Her neighbour, approaching her fence chewing a grass stalk, explained the police had paid a visit, half an hour before.

The trucker suddenly remembered commitments elsewhere and mumbled his apologies. Within seconds, he'd revved the engine and shouted goodbye. As the dust settled in his wake, she decanted hot coffee into an empty oilcan, wrapped the can in blankets and reached behind the stove where, that morning before leaving, she'd hidden the macaw's egg, bundled in newspaper. It was still warm as she placed it among snug woollen layers. She set about putting her kitchen back in order, every few hours stopping to boil water for the oilcan, and gently turn the egg. For four weeks, she kept this ritual, holding the egg to the light now and then to glimpse the hopeful dark spot. In the fifth week, the egg grew light and papery; she worried it was wasting away. She sat sorting batches of beans on the tabletop when tiny tap-tapping noises came from the makeshift incubator. The hatchling emerged — ashen-pink, pimply, and frosted with yolk-matted down. Its eyes bulged indigo under milky lids. With a feeble peep, it tipped forward onto its rubbery beak waiting, helpless, for her to do something.

The baby macaw was frail and impossible to please. She mashed endless combinations of corn and palm fruits, banana, and pounded beans, but it trembled and fell over more often than it ate. Foods that it liked on one day seemed not to pass muster on the next — she could ill afford the waste. Somehow, it survived this bald and vulnerable phase and began to open its eyes. Her own baby had to be kept far from the bird — he didn't have the co-ordination to avoid doing harm in his innocent attempts to make friends.

Over the weeks, she kept the chick carefully hidden. One night, exhausted and jumpy at the thought of the police returning, she wondered if she should have let the egg go cold. The nestling lifted its clownish head with blue feather-tufts poking through, gazed at her with white-rimmed eyes and she quickly repented the thought. When the last waxy feather-casings fell to reveal vivid hyacinth plumage, she felt surging maternal pride. The original cage was inadequate, now that the macaw was fledging and so she let it live free in the root-house. With no cassava harvest to store, she didn't need the space.

She cut some old branches and wedged them into convenient nooks to provide perches. Mauro's blunt old saw kept sticking, and as she cut the last branch, it skipped out of the groove, glancing off her left index finger. The rusty teeth raked a stinging graze; it oozed red.

She doubled over, cursing, "*Merda.*" Clamping the hand against her belly, "*Mer-dah.*"

The bird cocked its head, observing her. While she examined the damage, clear as the church bell and with great feeling, the macaw opined, "*Merrr-dah.*"

She spun around, still pressing on the cut, her mouth agape. The macaw blinked. Its charcoal tongue articulated the curse again. Nonchalantly then, it nibbled a piece of banana, delicately rotated with one claw. And so it was a mixture of mortification and wonder that spurred her to begin language lessons with her fine blue bird. Its first utterance had been a profanity, and if she couldn't quite erase that, she could at least expand its vocabulary to provide some alternatives. The bleeding at last stopped, and she fitted the final perch.

Useful, quotidian things came first to her mind, the points of the compass: *Norte, Sul, Este,* and *Oeste*; the days of the week. Her boy, not ready yet for words, still loved to bounce on her knee as she chanted syllables for the macaw. The bird was an eager student, apparently grateful for some stimulation other than stripping bark from perches. Few repetitions were required before it attempted each word, and the reproduction was comically perfect, boldly reproducing the accent and pitch of her voice. The macaw was reluctant to stop when domestic tasks called its teacher away, and sometimes, when she passed nearby with armfuls of laundry it would squawk words through the ventilation spaces in hope of extra conversation classes.

Mango season was approaching. She stood freckled by the shade of her few remaining trees, appraising the crop. The fat blushing fruits would bring a little income in December, a saving grace. She fetched a ladder and climbed into the canopy. Several fruits loosened and split on the cracked earth below. At close range, she saw black rot distorting the stems, burrowing into the hearts of the fruits. The harvest was shot.

Her gaze, blurred with tears, lifted to the horizon, an angry red line uninterrupted by trees. In the foreground, ranks of cornhusks rattled in their brittle furrows, last year's hopeful sowing. The spiteful sun turned everything to dust, and she knew she was beaten. You could make do for so long but without rain, without money, even love of the land is not enough. Her son began to cry and she climbed down to go to him.

Once more on the road to town, she made good time, reaching the suburbs before the sun's white malevolence levered itself above the buildings and crept down walls and blistered the streets. The central district was a lurching mass of heat and people. In a bar near the bus station, dark and besieged with flies, she made enquiries. The barmaid yelled through a vinyl curtain, never taking her eyes off the clouded mirror in which she was fixing her hair, then lazily motioned her head, indicating someone would come. Waiting by the entrance, watching street dogs nose through a torn litter sack, she held down the urge to run that swelled inside her chest. A man waddled from the bowels of the bar, hirsute belly jiggling beneath a misshapen vest. He rubbed his jaw, black with stubble, muttering the details to her. The truck leaves Thursdays, eight sharp, from the filling station out by the rail-track. She slid a banknote wad across the counter towards the barmaid's chipped claret nails. The man handed her a smudged corner of card for a receipt. She could bring two bags, no more.

He nodded at her son, who was peeking over her shoulder.

"The baby going?" A smile brightened his unshaven jowls for a moment, and then was gone. "So, only one bag."

While packing for the journey south, she sat briefly to train the macaw: names from her favourite soap operas, Bela Mama Martez and Eduardo Jobim, even short nursery rhymes. The bird repeated the days of the week with the perfect diction of an elocution student, and its favourite rhyme piped across the yard: 'My neighbour's hen lays brown speckled eggs. She lays one, she lays two, she lays three, she lays ten'. At night, she watched her son's chest rise and fall, his innocent babbling, and she cried and cursed at the things that lay ahead for them. Rio de Janeiro would be a little cooler — they'd see rain sometimes but she'd have no fields to sow, she'd exchange her farmhouse for a tin-roofed shack in a hill slum, work as a maid in some fancy apartment. Drugs flowed through those crooked slum-alleys, with violence panting close behind.

Remnants of night huddled around her turquoise house as she locked up. She took a long last look at the peeling walls. The macaw was huffy, squashed back into its old cage, feathers poking through at awkward angles, its fate uncertain. Her son was grouchy, having slept badly. She smoothed her hand over the door's worn wood, clenching her jaw to quell the grief coiled in her stomach. As she turned to begin the long trip south, weighed down with a holdall, the bird, her restless boy and a shapeless bale of fears, she prayed that one day she might return, and that the sun meanwhile, if it was the only good it did, might preserve her house. The macaw swung wildly as she picked up the cage, stuttering and scrambling to keep upright. She was losing her patience, losing her hold on the sobs that pressed at her throat. Something landed in her hair. Her first thought was locusts. A plague, years back, had driven her crazy, tangling in her hair. Another, bigger tap on her head. She shook her hair in irritation. But it wasn't quite like locusts. On the ground, other little percussions — and then she stopped, but didn't quite believe it. Fat raindrops splotching the dust at her feet. She watched, hypnotised. The rhythm gathered force, and soon she stood among swirling runnels. She turned her face to feel the drops sting her skin, to convince herself it wasn't a dream. Her son began to giggle, sending tickles down her back. Her dress was plastered to her skin and her hair to her scalp. The bird, hunched, fell silent. She took it into the root-house, and they sat listening to the full might of the gathering storm.

From her pocket she pulled out the truck docket — soggy now. She clasped it between her palms, frozen in hesitation. It had cost her almost all she had, and the bus would go without them if they were not there within an hour or two. Outside it was still too dark to judge the clouds. Before she married Mauro, there had been a break like this in the drought. They'd danced barefoot in the mud, and next day green sprouts nosed though parched crusts, leaves and flowers burst from branches that they'd thought dead. Soon brazen red earth was blanketed with green and everyone went out to till and sow in a fever. But there had been other rain showers that came only to tease and mock then pass on through, leaving hopeful seedlings to shrivel. She paced the cramped root-house floor. Rain could leave as suddenly as it came.

The macaw watched, blinking. Suddenly, it spoke, "*Norte.*"

She stopped pacing.

"*Norte,*" insisted the macaw, bashing its beak against the cage bars for emphasis.

Of all the words it knew, 'North' was all the dumb bird would say now. She looked out at the dawn light, struggling to show itself behind dense, molten clouds. There were days worth rolling in, she guessed. The sodden ticket to the south tore easily, and she went to pick up a hoe.

Next day as more rain doused the parched northeast, she took a break from sowing. Crossing her blood-red fields she propped the hoe against the root-house wall, pausing to listen to drips chiming from the eaves. Back in the scrub near the canyon where Mauro had trapped the macaw's mother, she released the bell-voiced fledgling who knew the points of the compass so well. Rain ran down her face and her son's and they smiled, watching hyacinth wings spread to fly north, and homewards.

PRETTY LUANA & ALL HER COLOURS

Zizí is scrubbing the sink with some vigour in time with a Marisa Monte CD. The ancient porcelain, crazed with grey veins, never looks truly clean, but it's satisfying to remove the worst of the accumulated grime. The sound of a key turning in the lock brings her to a halt and she waits, rubber gloves dripping, in the doorway, one bare foot on the tiled floor with suds between the toes, the other pressed to the inside of her knee.

Luana dumps her bags, all sorbet-coloured, in the hall.

"*Que dia!*" she says, and flops on the sofa, the mandarin neckline of her salon tunic climbing over her throat. "Oh, you're an angel, you cleaned the bathroom."

She looks past her flatmate at the cluttered room where they jostle for mirror-space each morning with a surprised-looking Polish girl and a moody Belarussian.

"If I wait for the other two to do it, we'll have white hair first." Zizí dries off the sink with a cloth.

"It's true, they don't seem to notice the mess — you just have to walk past their room to see that. My sister worked as an au pair in Florida for a year — you should have seen the state of that house."

Zizí laughs, spreading a clean cloth out with her feet at the bathroom entrance. She goes to pour some squash at the kitchen counter and brings a glass for Luana.

"How was work?"

"*Aiee!* This awful old senhora: she lives to complain. It's always, 'Stupid girl, faster, hurry hurry.' Then if you hurry,

93

'Useless girl, you missed a bit.' And the slightest little nick and she's all, 'Yeoowww, *aiee*, you hurt me.'"

"*Sério?*"

"She's mean. Feet like pigs' trotters too. Yeuch. None of the others will do her pedicure, they leave her for me. Then my boss is saying I have to work more hours, but she can't pay me yet. I don't know what to do — the rent's due."

Zizí shakes her head. "Yeah. I came here with all these ideas I could save up, send money home, and still be back for Carnaval, but here I am months later and not one penny saved."

"The cost of living's impossible. I thought everyone here earned at least a *Salário Mínimo*." Luana picks at multicoloured specks of nail polish on her tunic. "How's the bar?"

"Oh, the same. My lecherous boss tried to feel my ass last night. Made me stay late to clean up the toilets, then says he doesn't have the money for the extra hours I did this month because someone owes him money. And I have to pay him £10 for the 'uniform'."

"That crummy tee shirt? *Que idiota.* It's not your problem if somebody owes him."

"The guy's clueless."

"I felt so homesick today, missing my little *Mamãe*."

"Me too. The climate doesn't help. You never see the sun, just a tiny candle, way in the distance."

"And this is almost midsummer — it's incredible more people don't go crazy or emigrate." Luana circles her finger at her temple.

"They do — it's only us gringos and the most crazy locals left. Everybody else went to Spain. Hey..." Zizí springs from the sofa and starts opening the kitchen cupboards. "I'm going to make rice and beans — homely food to cheer us up."

"Oh yeah, let's have *caipirinhas* too, that'll liven up the evening. Come on, we can get all life's necessities at the corner shop."

The girls walk in the narrow aisles of the strip-lit convenience store, picking up bulk packs of rice and beans, some limes, a papery garlic bulb. "Don't think they'll have *cachaça*," Zizi mutters.

"If they did, it'd be with the fancy imports, £25 a bottle." Luana cranes her neck, scanning the liquor shelf.

"It makes me laugh — like those Havaianas flip flops we saw for £20 in the mall: standard issue for every maid in São Paulo, and one step up from being a barefoot ragamuffin."

"Look, this white rum would do." The clear bottle is reflected in Luana's lilac-rimmed eyes.

"It's the right price anyway."

They pile their rations on the counter and pay the shopkeeper, who pauses from stacking Lottery tickets into a display box. She smiles serenely, in her straining purple sari. Horizontal creases form through the red dot on her forehead, like clouds across the moon.

Back in the flat, Zizi slices garlic. She puts it with the beans and some water into the rickety pressure cooker she bought from Oxfam in her first weeks in Britain. A symbolic purchase, it was an effort to kill her homesickness through food. Luana quarters vivid limes and pounds them in a glass with sugar.

"You know it's ages since I had *caipirinha*. These are going to taste heavenly." She takes ice lumps from the freezer and fills the glasses.

"Here." She passes one to Zizí, drizzling rum over the ice.

"Mm-mn." Zizí pinches her earlobe in appreciation. She chops more garlic. "You make them really good — even without proper sugar-rum."

"My Tio Paulo taught me. The secret is to crush some of the lime skin — it lets the oils out."

The pressure cooker valve begins to spin like an enraged genie, spurting out steam. The flatmates down another *caipirinha* each.

"Ah, I'm almost forgetting that shitty job." Luana pulls the pins out of her hair and goes to change her tunic for a tee shirt.

"Rum's the best medicine," Zizí calls after her. "What would you be doing back home on a Thursday night?"

Luana comes back, brighter now in her aqua shirt, stretching out on the sofa. "Oh, at my aunt's, eating barbeque, or..." She looks, disconsolate, at the ceiling, "... doing nails and hair for friends. You?"

Zizí, in the bathroom doorway, is smoothing out the frizz in her curls with some oil. "Um, I could be helping *Mamãe* stitch something for a customer, or if we were at the beach, playing volley."

"Let's not talk about that."

"You're right. No point in thinking of all those people — we'll only miss them more. Did you check the paper for jobs?"

"No — d'you buy it?"

Zizí lobs the folded newspaper into Luana's lap. "Don't think there's much."

"Hey, there's a salon job going at Jenners. Ah, but you have to have an H — N — D. What's that?"

"Some kind of diploma, I think."

"The kind I don't have." Luana sucks on an ice cube, scanning the classified pages, occasionally stopping to read out an ad in a slow, discouraged voice. "Zi — what's that smell?"

"*Aiee*, no! The beans." She dives across to the stove, wrenching the pot off the heat, but inside, instead of the velvety stew smelling of home whose warmth they have so anticipated, a desiccated crust lines the bottom of the pot, the beans exploded or shrunken in their skins. The muddy purée cracks in places revealing blackened metal underneath. The girls feel their stomachs sink in disappointment. Luana's first thought is to make more rum cocktail.

But Zizi is already pulling out bread rolls from the cupboard. She cuts them open, stuffs slices of ham between the doughy halves, wraps them in kitchen paper. "Come on, let's go out."

Down the North Bridge they walk, in silence. Overhead it's cloudy, as usual, but the air is warm, humid. Pigeons pecking in the gutters scatter into the sky as they approach. Wine-painted double-decker buses roar by, reflected in shop windows. They turn into Chambers Street and down past the libraries to Princes Street Gardens.

Luana bites into her ham roll, "Mm — *que delícia!*" kissing her fingertips in mock ecstasy.

Zizi rolls her eyes, pecking at the sorry-looking sandwiches, a floury substitute for the comfort food they had planned.

"Maybe there'll be a great job in the paper next week." She links arms with Luana. "Just imagine, a boss who lets you go to the bathroom once every six hours."

97

"A wage that's enough to buy some fried chicken just once every little month." Luana says, brushing crumbs from her shirt, the colour of swimming pools.

That was almost the beginning of the game where they imitate their fathers' tales of exaggerated hardship, usually taken to ludicrous extremes, but today they haven't the enthusiasm. People in the gardens are wearing tee shirts, sitting on the grass eating, laughing as if it were thirty-five degrees. A group of teenagers share a tartan blanket; on one corner, two girls paint each other's nails.

Zizí says, "I have an idea. We can get out of those terrible jobs."

"*Hein, hein.* Your last idea sounded so good, but unfortunately, *minha senhora...*"

"Hey, you didn't need to mention the beans." Zizí pokes Luana in the ribs. "Anyway, this one's better: we'll open our own shop." She is all smiles, her hands pressed together, awaiting her friend's indulgence.

Luana gives her a tired look, barely disguising her disappointment. Lazy raindrops begin to splotch the tarmac. People cluster under trees with their rugs, like refugees. "But *como*? We hardly can pay the rent, let alone buy premises..."

"Wait, don't think about that yet. I can sew stuff. They don't have tailoring for ordinary people here — only for the *ricos*. I'll make bikinis, dresses, shirts; cool Brazilian stuff, the kind people go crazy for here. And you have a great eye for colours, right? You can do the layout of the place, make it look good — and do nails and salon stuff too. Your own clients — you could send the rude ones home."

"Yeah... but Zí, where? There's no place we could afford."

"There's the one downstairs. I'm sure that miserable landlord would be glad to rent it, since it looks like a bat cave."

"It's full of pigeon shit, probably not even habitable."

"The flat wasn't much better, but we scrubbed it up."

"He'll put the price up as soon as we show interest. You know how it goes."

"If he's smart, he'll let it out for something rather than leave it empty."

"I dunno. We could give it a try, but even if it was £100 a month, I don't see how I could..."

"We'll ask him."

"And don't you need permits and so on? I mean we're not exactly citizens..."

"There'll be a way around it, some little trick."

Luana laughs, "You're such a Brasileira!"

They walk on through the gardens and up the steps towards the West End.

Zizí is still caught up in her idea. "Just imagine it: your own salon chair and my clothes in a cool little shop. It would be unique."

Luana lets herself get lost in the dream for a minute. The rain falls in the same lethargic rhythm.

"I suppose it would be fun. Anything's better than what we do now. I could get *Mamãe* to send me some 'Dara' nail colours. No one else has those here."

"That's it. We can call the shop, 'Pretty Luana and All Her Colours'."

"Hah, I like it! But I think your name needs to be in there too. How about 'Luana, Crazy Zizí and All the Colours of Brazil'? There wouldn't be enough room on the banner."

They develop the theme, nearing the end of the street.

Luana looks wistfully towards the spire of St John's Church as they near the corner of Princes Street.

Zizi grabs her arm. "Hey, I have it. There's a market here."

Luana follows her gaze, across the churchyard flagstones towards the graveyard below. "In the cemetery?"

"No, dumb girl, on the patio there, at weekends."

Luana frowns.

"See. We don't need a shop. A market stall can't be so expensive." She turns to Luana, her eyes sparkling. "How about it?"

They look at the puddled space where vendors will gather on Saturday, spreading out their candles, candyfloss and bean-filled frogs. A chink in the molten sky lets through a spear of sunshine. Luana notices a rainbow has spun itself across the city, arching from behind the Castle, painting colour through the grey, and dipping towards the horizon somewhere beyond the monuments of Calton Hill. And just then, in that narrow moment, the weather doesn't seem so bad.

Urban Poetry

The twins inhabited doorways, deserted rail-yards and parking lots after dark. They took out aerosols and rollers, covered their shoes in plastic bags, and faced the wall, the blank canvas. Through the night, in quiet synchrony they filled the wall with beauty and colour: scenes of family love, people in transit, of death and a nation's aching social injustices. As dawn threaded a thin finger between the parking lot's concrete blocks it found the artists tired but happy, putting finishing touches to their mural — a spray of white bringing life to eyes, a slogan more poetry than polemic. Finally, the tag that identified the work as theirs, a spiky, alien, artful signature, illegible, yet quite familiar. They walked home, stopping at a bakery for coffee, red rays punching across the cityscape.

The car park manager, arriving at work, frowned and wondered how much grey paint to order this time.

Forgotten Tigers of Rio de Janeiro

Papai was a tiger. But he never roar. He silent an strong, an he can be stealthy an clever too, when he have to be. He defend us little one, an all the weaklin in the pack, with great courage, so much it becomin his name: Coragem. An, when he have to do it, he defend himself too, brave an sure — an so noble that everybody roun get struck dumb. An he have his stripes. Oh sure, hard workin get him his stripes

In the days when Papai live in Rio, he work for a Portugee; big fat planter with one big fancy house up by the Petropolis road. The Portugee buy him in the Valongo market, 'cause Papai is beautiful with so dark, dark skin an long, lean muscle, so good white teeth, an strong, broad feet. The Siqueira plantation all cane, hunder acre of it, an Papai work hard, so hard, an soon get some reputation for bein good worker, who can plant all the rows he get give, an never be tire. But toilin don't earn him any better life. Seem like harder you work, harder they beat you. Papai he never complain, jus keep right on workin. What can you do? In them day, slave is slave, master is master. Slave keep on, keep on workin til they back break, an master is sit roun all day gettin fat from cane money. Even some slave arrange slave for themselves. Even carpenter get helpers to carry the tools aroun. Rio hardly can wake up in the mornin without slave. This the kind a city she is back then.

After all the years of plantin cane, burnin cane, cuttin an cookin it, Papai stronger than anybody. No matter how many beatin he get, he back in the field at daybreak. An the Portugee, he so dumb he boast all about his slave who never get tire, no matter how many cane row he lay out. Soon, this the gossip you hearin all roun the rich neighbourhood — my Papai, Coragem, jus a poor slave, but famous all the same. All the Europeen noble an the merchant hear of him, an the rich Carioca too. They start lookin at they own slave, the housemaid an the farmhand, the gardener an they laundry girl, an they see how they workin, sweatin, half fallin down with overwork, but all the same they get jealous. They want for themself a slave that never tire. They want Coragem.

Rio a small place then, not like today, so the tittle-tattlin don't take long to work its way aroun, even as far as the Royal Court. This why the Portugee so dumb for boastin. 'Cause if Dona Carlota, the Princesa, schemin in her head that she want somethin, she always would get it. Many rich Senhores have rue the time an the money they spend makin they home an they thing all so beautiful, for seem like more beautiful they get, the more temptation for the Princesa. One French planter lose his mansion up on Tijuca hill to her. Furnish with fine marble - ship from Paris, it was, an silk from the Goa. Barely is the silken drape hang an the royal order come to move out. Princesa have other mansion, three, four aroun town, maybe, but she want this one too. See, it have the best view. Even a rich Senhor can never say no to the Princesa. An so it was when her Majesty come gallopin roun the Portugee's plantation, hopin for a glimpse of Coragem, her eyes all full up with hungerin an covetin, the master know he have lose his best slave. When the workers tell him Princesa come ridin on his land, he curse his boastin mouth. The plantation master heavy with sorrows as Papai get take to the Royal Mansion at Botafogo.

The Portugee folk don't much like washin themself. Nor the French, an the English jus as bad. Everybody know that — especial the slave who lives close up beside them. They know by the smell how they don't have much to do with soap. Washin a thing for low class folks, the rich Europee all say. Refine people never touch nothin dirty, so they never needin wash. The plantation labourer always is washin, even if all they got is a bit rain in a ol tin. Papai know these thing, but even he get shock by the terrible ways he find at Dona Carlotas palace. He waitin to be put out for fieldwork, but it never happen. The rich white in downtown Rio get tire of the stench of they own shit, real bad in our hot Carioca summer, so they contrivin a way to take it far from under they nose. They pile the shit on the backs of slave, like walkin filth trap, see? So the problem get solve. This what the Princesa bring Coragem to do. He must run down the beach carryin a big wooden crate an tip the foulin in the sea. The filth-water leak out down his shoulder, burn his black skin white. Them slave that carry the foulin-crate, all get stripe with white, an everybody callin them Tigers.

Coragem believe the Royal House might bring better livin for him. Some slave at the Court get work carryin the Prince Regente, Dom João, in his chair roun Rio. Real fat an heavy this Dom João, but for eight strong men, that some easy work. They wearin red jalecas, lookin so fine. Papai think maybe he work at liftin chair too. But Dona Carlota some fierce Patroa. When thing not just how she want, she curl her thin lip, an order vicious lashin. Some day she make her footmen beat people in the street only cause they din bow an throw themself down when she pass by. People say she have so much ill-will for bein Spanish, but no matter the reason, Papai, when he see the beatins, know his punishin soon get more often, more force to every lashin an more hateful. So he resolve his mind an he run away.

I don't know for sure if Papai know right where he go when he flee from the palace, through the back street of Botafogo an to the swamps of Guanabara Bay. Maybe he have a plan, maybe he just run in a fever, anythin to get escapin Princesa an her spite. But bein clever like a tiger, an bein call Coragem, he find his way through the bog-lands full a bloodsuckers to a quilombo in the wood. He have nothin to carry, just the trouser he standin in. The other runaway slave an freed-man in this quilombo treat him wary at first. He have to live at the edges, nearby but not in that slave camp. He have to bring fish an hunt beast an bring to the edge for the freedman to eat. He have to show he clever an strong, not some ill-willin enemy. In time, they leavin Papai come inside the quilombo. They call him Tigre, cause he only one tiger in the camp, though plenty livin still in the city, workin, sure, an never stoppin, with the burnin filth stripin they shoulders. After some years, maybe eight, maybe ten, Tigre, who was call Coragem truly, come to be head of the camp. They all get by with huntin an fishin, findin scraps an plantin some little bit corn an cane in a patch clear from the wood. They live some hard life sure, but no lashins, an no carryin shit for no patroa. Have to be stealthy an look out for the Delegados who come raidin now an then again. They got to move the camp, stay ahead of the Police who always say the quilombolas was bad people, people that stealin an killin an all kind a law-breakin.

One sore day Delegados come catch Tigre, my Papai, Coragem, sayin he steal cane from a barge. Wasn true, for Papai and all the camp grow they own cane in the little field, but police say he stealin anyway, so he have to go to the Forum in front of the Sheriff an all the counsels. Well people say that slave or quilomobola in a court is good as provin guilty before any word speak, an they say the jail so hard to run from, not even the ants can scape. The news get all roun Rio, high society Senhores remembrin Coragem, an how strong he work, and what happen him all these year. Papai don't know what to do. But Coragem is his name for good reason an he feel his tiger stripe burnin, so he say he will climb those Forum step to show them how honest man lookin. Now my Papai no good in readin, never write even his own name, but he practise everythin he plan on sayin. To himself at night an in his prayin, he practise them over an over. He say to himself, if I don't speak the truth, I am not Coragem.

In the Forum, the counsel dress in black like vulture, an Coragem wear a white shirt stitch by a girl in the quilombo. He don't follow all they say, but he speak his truth when they turn to him. Another day in the Forum an the same happen over again. Papai get in the newspaper. All Rio readin bout a tiger in the court, sayin truly he have courage for who ever see slave standin up before a Sheriff. But at night, he lie down quiet in that cell, practisin his word an tellin his story. On the third day, the vulture enter back in the court. Papai stand straight in the corner waitin to say his story. But Sheriff speak to counsel, tellin them be quick. They tellin some lie, then Sheriff tell Papai he must swear truth an tell Senhor Sheriff what happen.

Papai lookin the counsel-men in they eye.

"Stealin is crime," he say. "It say so in the Bible an must say too in the law book."

Coragem look at Sheriff too, then. "Stealin when a man take thing away from another person that don't belong."

He look aroun the courtroom, his heart beatin quick as poppin corn. "Well I don't know who takin sugarcane from a barge at Iguaçu, but I know a baby girl on Siqueira Estate who have her Papai snatch away from her."

An that baby girl he speak about is me.

"Her Daddy steal away from her by a High Society Sin'ya."

That jus how slave talkin then: 'Sin'ya' and 'Ya Ya', an never sayin 'Senhora'. Coragem was speakin of the Princesa, owner of all Brazil an more, who take every thing she want. He never speak her name, but everybody know it. The Sheriff put his frown on an get impatient face. He tell my Papai to 'save breath for answerin question'.

But Coragem say, "That baby girl is my daughter. The Sin'ya who grab me from that place takin that girl's Papai from her like somebody take sugar cane from the barge: no askin, no payin. That call stealin — isn it so, my lord? The Sin'ya take me like some bundle a cane, but a person never can be takin like he a thing."

Jus then ol Sheriff eye is change, lookin real careful at Coragem now.

Papai turn to one counsel, "Can somebody steal you? No, 'cause person is differin from cane. A person can never be steal."

An Coragem don't waste time waitin for answer. "Is slave differin? If a slave is own, he jus a thing, an one thing can never get up an steal another thing. But if slave a person, he have rights — to a roof shelterin his head, to be treatin jus an right by the law, to food an all the thing every person need for livin."

Now the folk in the court all whisperin and agitatin.

"I never read any law book, but everybody know a fair hearin in court is depen on proofs. An where the proofs to say Coragem is at the river that night takin cane that don't belong?"

Coragem is no professor, but he try to speak something he know is true. Some truths he feel burn in his heart, an in his stripes. But he don't have fancy words an he fearin the Sheriff an those vulture an the powers they get. Papai don't have much, but he have taste freedom these last year an he know Senhor Sheriff can take it from him.

The vulture makin huddle now, cluck-cluckin. They come speak with Sheriff, who breathe deep an get strange, weary look.

He say, "We here to speak about the crime of stealing cane from a boat, not hear high-conceivin ideas about all the history of law an Brazil."

An one vulture step forward, face grey an wrinkle, an he speak without lookin at Coragem.

"Proofs you say? Well Senhor Sé Quiroga swear in his statement that he did indeed see a person, more less the height of you, lingerin by the cane barge, night of the crime. This Senhor much esteem'd in Rio Society, from one very old planter family, a trusty witness." The vulture look, noddin, at the court. "And more," he say. "You, the accuse, a fugitive. Once a labourer, belongin to Siqueira plantation.

Later a runaway, hidin from your patroa, slippin from the law, livin in the woods like some savage. Jus the kind of character who may have no scruple, who have reason to steal."

An Coragem feel his heart weight down, like a rock tie aroun it. He have no word to match the counsel.

The door of the Forum open an Coragem thinkin everybody must leave so Sheriff can think over the punishins. But no person move. Coragem don't believe his eye but theres ol boss Portugee walkin in the court. The vulture unnatural silent an everybody stare. Portugee walk heavy an slow, bow before Sheriff an shake hand with the vulture one by one. He stand before the court an speak of my Papai, sayin marvellous thing — but all of it truth. He tell how he honest an trusty, sorely missin on plantation since he get take from there, an how Papai hard-workin an never would steal. An Papai start shakin, look between Sheriff an the planter, not knowin if the Portugee want his slave back or Sheriff want him a prisoner. Either way he lose his freedom an what can be worse?

But jus then a merciful thing happen, the Sheriff tell Papai to go. At first he don't believe his ear, but Sheriff tellin him again. Then in the spring sunshine, in his white press shirt, Coragem walk out of court, tall an smilin thankful.

HOLY ANTS

News of our little Bom Jesus miracle spread like influenza. Alabaster eyes don't cry. Everyone knows that. And yet we all saw it, real salt tears rolling down putty-pale cheeks. Granny Álvaro crossed herself, unsteady upon the mango-tree roots that stitched the square, and someone ran to get Padre Silvano das Flores. The old man came, woozy from his afternoon nap. The crowd parted. Padre Silvano scrambled for his spectacles, patting every pocket but the right one, finally wiggling the tortoiseshell frames over his ears. Squinting, stooping double almost, he peered under the Virgin's modestly inclined brow, reached out a finger to dab her cheeks and taste for salt.

Padre Silvano das Flores declared the tears indeed seemed miraculous. "But the miracle of Divine Love is best witnessed in God's House."

The crowd, murmuring excitedly, heard only the word 'miracle'. Padre Silvano sat down in the shade, blotting his forehead with a handkerchief. Granny Álvaro scurried home to bring *cafezinhos* with extra sugar for everyone. That night a candlelight vigil drew confetti clouds of moths. The villagers gazed on the Virgin and, faces aglow in the quivering light, relived the wonder of the Tears in animated whispers.

First on the scene next morning was the local hack, camera lopsided on puny shoulders. Granny Álvaro tut-tutted, seeing his cigarette butts dropped in the dust. In next day's *Diário* , his shots — small and smudgy — did no justice to the gravity of the event. Soon the out-of-town pilgrims started rolling in, knitted together at the elbows, inching overawed towards Her.

That was how Granny found her new vocation — as unofficial curator of a National Treasure. She could see the shrine from her yard, and quietly assumed the duties of sweeping, straightening subsided candles and clearing away over-ripe mangoes unceremoniously splotched in the Holy lap. She loved to tell her eyewitness account of Maria Lacrimosa's Miracle Tears to those who came seeking blessings. Serena, her eldest grandchild, called round after school to help serve *cafezinhos* to the visitors. Granny smiled in thousands of photographs, and began to sing a lot.

Not everyone was happy with our Madonna's spreading fame. The Padre, at first overjoyed at his parishioners' newfound reverence for the shrine, grew cynical of the 'Faith Tourists' clustering in the square. Few worshippers visited his Church of Our Lady of Bom Jesus anymore, where the Salvador road bridged the river. The Bishop, hearing of dwindling congregations, suggested Padre Silvano's sermons had lost their zeal. The Padre ordered the removal of the Virgin. A team of green-clad council workers dug up her concrete base one morning, before the first pilgrims arrived. They unscrewed Our Lady Lacrimosa from her post, wrapped her in tarpaulin, and, crossing themselves, wheeled her away. She was secured with a heavy padlock in a shed next to Granny Álvaro's place, beneath an ancient cashew tree. Granny was livid, then inconsolable. That day the pilgrims found no one to explain, just a small hole among the mango roots. Serena grew worried about her grandmother, who stayed in bed a lot while ants rampaged in her garden, cutting the cassava plants to lace.

Padre Silvano's plan did little to revive attendance at his church by the river. He surveyed the empty pews, a lonely figure in faded gowns. Serena tried to lure Granny back to her vegetables with various appeals, the weeds were waist-high, the bean pods ready to split. But nothing could rouse her. The girl pleaded with the Padre, but he wouldn't hear of the statue returning. He still hoped to swell his congregation with pilgrims seeking real spiritual sustenance, disillusioned with the showier end of divine manifestation.

One day, Serena brought a leaf to show Granny Álvaro, who sat mute by the window staring out at the garden that was once her passion.

"Look, Granny, how weird."

The old woman would not look. Serena, sighing, put the leaf down and went to brew coffee.

"I haven't seen anything so strange since the day of Our Lady's Tears," she called nonchalantly from the kitchen.

When she came out carrying cups, the leaf was in Granny's crooked hands, turning in the light from the windowpane. Tiny holes let pinpricks of white light through its waxy tissue.

Granny's rheumy eyes resolved a pattern, and a slow smile returned to her face.

"Where did you find this, child?" It was no ordinary pattern that she saw.

"Under the cashew tree."

Captive or no, the Madonna's power was unstoppable, and now Granny could show them. She sprung up to fetch her broom, handling it more like a delicate archaeological tool than a cleaning implement. She was gone for quite a while, sifting leaves under the cashew tree near the imprisoned statue.

"They can take away our shrine," she would tell pilgrims, "but they can't suppress the Loving Influence of Our Lady Maria Lacrimosa."

That evening Granny Álvaro gathered in ripe bean-pods from her garden, humming gently.

Bound in tight purple, Senhora Pasquale's huge bosom danced a precarious rhythm, ba-ba-dham, ba-ba-dhum, as she rolled steadily along the dirt lane towards the square. Her feet, keeping a quite different rhythm, wobbled in wedge-heeled sandals whose straps latticed her ankles into doughy diamonds.

"Oh, Dona Al-va-roh?" the teacher called from the yard, her wheezy voice piping in through the window.

Drying her hands on an embroidered towel, Granny greeted Senhora Pasquale with a kiss. She poured coffee, but the teacher was impatient, her eyes darting around for evidence of miracles. Too kind to make her suffer suspense, the old lady led her outside to where ants in looping lines carried sails of cut leaf up the trunk of the cashew. Granny Álvaro swiped a few leaves around with her broom. Not every one was patterned, rather one in every few. She found a big red leaf, formidably punctured. A continuous line of tiny holes formed a clear profile of the Madonna at prayer.

"It must be those blasted ants. Perhaps they're on the side of the Good after all," cackled Granny.

Senhora Pasquale caught her breath, looking from the leaf to the padlocked door in the shadow of the tree, behind which Maria Lacrimosa languished.

113

"*Meu Jesus!*" she marvelled, rubbing chubby fingers over the perforations. Granny went on leaf-combing, inspired.

"If the Senhora doesn't mind..." began the teacher, "I feel this matter must go all the way to the Bishop."

Granny picked a sprig of rosemary, wordlessly put it behind her ear. They would be bypassing the irreverent Padre Silvano and his jealous padlocks.

"But first we should get it verified by someone — a person of letters — to add weight to the discovery." She held Granny's hand for a long time at the gate before departing with some miraculous leaves in a paper bag, and a little more levity in her step.

The bus to Vitória was hot and crowded. The driver's rosary beads clack-clacked against the windscreen as he cursed potholes. Senhora Pasquale fanned her ticket serenely and thought of holy things. Bumping and lurching along, the good teacher began to see that God had plans for her. Though modest Bom Jesus, and a grandmother's humble yard, was the setting for the 'Perforations Miracle', it was surely intended for a professional woman like herself to see its significance, and take its message to the world. The People must know. She frowned at the gravity of her calling. As they trundled through a neighbouring town, she noticed the TV Globo office. It would be an easy matter on her return, she mused with growing conviction, to alight a few stops early and find a journalist, so beginning her evangelical mission.

The heat was punishing, a trial of faith, thought Senhora Pasquale, as she reached the concrete plaza of the Agriculture Faculty. In the foyer she studied a framed gallery of teaching staff, a little intimidated by the rows of erudite faces. A guard in grey came ambling over.

"*Bom dia*. Professor..." She circled her finger over the photos, "...Santos?" The only way to choose in the end, was by a sympathetic-sounding name.

"The insect-rearing facility, Senhora." The guard gestured across the dusty concourse to a low white building. Senhora Pasquale shuddered.

Her timid knocks went unanswered, thrumming noises came from inside.

She called, "*Alô*, Professor Santos?"

A man appeared, blinking a little in the sun splicing the floor. He beckoned her into his realm of buzzing air-conditioners. She explained the entire Miracle Tears and Perforations saga without pausing for breath, angling her head in gentle imploring movements.

Professor Santos' brow rumpled. He examined the leaves. The join-the-dots praying Virgins were plain to see, despite cracks beginning in the desiccated tissue.

"Senhora..." The Professor cleared his throat. "How do you believe these patterns were created?"

She stammered a little. "Well, um, they appeared in a very Holy Place... where a... miraculous icon is stored. The only hole-forming creatures there are ants. We thought perhaps the insects were... moved by some greater force." She flushed a little.

He pursed his lips, nodding. "Come and meet our laboratory pets."

Back in Bom Jesus, Granny Álvaro sang, busily weeding among her bean rows. It was the ideal spot from which to greet pilgrims and passing locals and show them the tattooed leaves. People were disappointed not to find the weeping Madonna, but left deeply consoled by the

115

perforated cashew leaves. Vegetable-matter portraiture, after all, surely belonged to a rarer class of miracle than tearful icons.

At Vitória University Myrmecology Unit, Professor Santos led Senhora Pasquale into a dim room where, in glass chambers on shelves, hundreds of ants laboured, cleaning their nests, shifting leaves. Her eyes glowed at the sight of such industry.

"They make holes in leaves. You are right," the professor said.

"All moved by a common purpose," she whispered, smiling.

"Perhaps. But look closely. How are they cutting the leaf tissue?"

Senhora Pasquale's breath clouded the glass. So much life, clambering over itself, now made her a little queasy. The ants started at leaf borders, carving ragged lines, like children scissoring shapes from old magazines. He held a magnifying lens before her eyes, bringing her suddenly face-to-face with an egg-sized head. She recoiled slightly, unprepared for such intimacy with hooky amber mandibles, slicing a rose leaf.

"It's kind of... methodical, like... garden shears."

"Exactly. They cut lines, like shears. They don't have the right anatomical configuration to make your perforations, pretty as they are. I'm afraid ants are not your number one suspects."

Senhora Pasquale's eyebrows swooped together, forming an angry pinch. "But these ants are perhaps a different species, Professor." She looked him squarely in the eye, one educated person to another, as she spoke the word 'species'.

Professor Santos led her to a bench cluttered with Petri dishes and flasks. "Here, look under the 'scope."

He adjusted the plate to take one of the Senhora's crinkly leaves. She looked down the eyepiece at its burnished surface, magnificent in such close detail.

"See the shape of the holes? Concave, yes? Dipping inwards? But look at the very centre, they curve back a little. Whatever punctured the leaf was pulled out."

Senhora Pasquale turned to face him. He had not gone so far as to suggest a fraudster at work with a tailor's pin, but she understood the implication. Her face burned, she felt like one of her own miscreant pupils.

"These holes, Senhora, were made with some smooth, sharp instrument. I'm afraid no species of ant has such piercing apparatus in its mouthparts, or elsewhere."

"But it's the only explanation — there is no other leaf-perforating creature there."

"Is this tree under twenty-four hour guard?" He gave her a hawk-like look.

She lowered her eyes.

And, raising his arms in a gesture of helplessness, he added, "sorry" for he knew she had come a long way to verify her miracles.

The road back to the station was interminable, her steps dragged. Senhora Pasquale stopped for coconut water, grateful for the shade of the vendor's umbrella. The cool drink revived her fury. What a fool she'd been to come here, 'Professor Santos' indeed. All his talk of 'suspects'. They had witnessed a miracle, not a crime.

"The Pope will have something to say," she told the bewildered coconut seller, handing him the empty green nut. She waddled off towards the bus station.

The indignant teacher descended the bus in Pires and went to find a listener at the TV Globo office. Milene, the Local Affairs Correspondent, punctuated Senhora Pasquale's story with attentive nods, her dark eyes moving fluidly.

She scribbled shorthand, exclaiming, "You're taking the leaves to Rome?" as the teacher repeated her conviction about His Holiness the Pope.

She examined the leaves, noted who had found them and when. She agreed to come the next day to see the miraculous ants.

Senhora Pasquale trudged a much-decelerated rhythm along the lane to Granny Álvaro's place as dusk settled in. She collapsed into a chair and told the old woman of her adventures. Granny shook her head steadily at the scientist's cynical verdict.

The teacher wagged a finger at Serena, emerging quietly from her bedroom to pour some cashew juice. "You look tired, sweetheart."

Granny's face lit up at talk of the TV crew, and she began checking her coffee supplies, straightening lacy covers on her chairs.

Late the next afternoon, Granny smoothing her apron, Senhora Pasquale reapplying lipstick, the film crew showed up sudden and brusque like a cyclone. They scoured the yard filming all the worst leaf specimens, and were gone. Watching Granny's ancient TV set the following evening, the women made impatient comments about the other items on Globo News: coffee markets in freefall, the price of a sack less than twenty years ago.

"So tell us something we don't know," huffed Senhora Pasquale.

When it seemed the broadcast would end without mention of miracles, the newscaster finally announced the ants.

"Serena! Come, dear," called Granny.

But it was not Granny's face that appeared next.

"Professor Santos," began correspondent Milene's voice. "Explain why you think perhaps the patterns in these perforated leaves are not what they seem."

The ant expert held a cork with a bradawl protruding from it. He demonstrated how pushing sharp metal into a leaf would produce holes just like those found in the Bom Jesus leaves.

"...not anatomically possible they were made by ants," he concluded.

Milene nodded earnestly and spoke to camera.

"She's taking the leaves to Rome?" Professor Santos' final words delivered with a dubious shrug. "Well, I hope they enjoy the trip."

They sat in stunned silence as the 8.00 p.m. soap opera began. Serena took the cups to the kitchen and went outside. No one had much to say after that. Senhora Pasquale departed well before nine. Granny took out a chair and sat in the moonlight watching the ants' winding chain gangs. After a while she noticed it was past time to send her granddaughter home, and went to call her. She found sandals stationed together by the kitchen door, but no sign of Serena. Guessing she must have fallen asleep, Granny stole towards the back room like a cat. As she peeked around the door, there was a clattering sound. The curtains billowed up in a ruffle, a fallen chair settled, and, rolling in diminishing arcs on the floor, was a cork speared with a curious spike.

The old woman stood in the doorway, silently observing the scene.

"Just as the scientist thought." She shook her head wistfully. "He's a smart one."

Eventually Serena came slinking in by the front door, shoulders hunched defensively. Granny took a perforated leaf from her bedside table and held it to the lamp.

"You are gifted, dear. You must have spent hours on these. They're quite a work of art."

"I'm a deceiver."

Granny looked at her, perturbed, and sat down.

"I didn't do it to trick anyone," Serena went on. "But you were so down after they took away Maria Lacrimosa."

The old woman gave a heavy sigh of realisation. She stooped to gather more leaves from the floor. Together they picked up the chair and the instrument of deception.

Granny Álvaro examined the cork. It was one of her darning needles driven into the centre. "You were trying to cheer up your old Granny, *querida*. If that's not the work of God, I don't know what is," she said, smoothing the counterpane. "It doesn't matter much whether those patterns were yours or the ants'. Only Senhora Pasquale and I said it was the ants. If only she hadn't gone to Vitória ..."

"What a mess." Serena's brow crinkled, her chin puckered, "A Professor, the TV! And now she's going to Rome."

"Oh, Little One, there's no need for anyone to know. We'll persuade Senhora Pasquale it was all a fuss over nothing. Maybe the little ants got tired, hmm?" She traced the dark semi-circles under Serena's eyes with her thumb. "There's no proof. Who'll believe her?"

"Wouldn't that be lying, Granny? I'll go to hell."

"Hush, 'course not. We'll let everyone remember it as another Bom Jesus miracle. It'll do no harm — sometimes people are a little... kinder when they believe in miracles." Granny smoothed Serena's satin hair. "Let the scientists see a confused old woman who thought she saw something in the leaves."

Granny caught her reflection in the windowpane. "I doubt they'd be impressed by our Maria Lacrimosa's Tears either." She rose to boil the kettle. "But people will still travel from all over to visit Bom Jesus," she continued from the kitchen doorway, "even with Our Maria locked away. There were scenes of wonder beneath that tree, after all." The kettle whistled. "And I'll bring them coffee and tell them about the Tears."

Serena opened the door to the garden for her grandmother carrying the steaming kettle.

"Meanwhile, I'll teach those cursed ants to cut my cassava plants, miracle or no. See if I don't — Mother Maria, forgive me."

THE CAPTAIN'S WOMAN

Wake up, Carmina Bonita.
Wake up and set the coffee to brew —
The day is already dawning, and
The police already on the trail.

For anyone who dared to say that Carmina Bonita was not blessed, whether by nature or by God, with the charm suggested by her nickname, there was always the persuasive fist of Ferrinho.

Necessity was what brought them together. Getúlio Amadeu da Silva, better known as Ferrinho (for his heart of iron, some say), found himself horseless in the vicinity of Three Rivers farm, having lost his best mare to gangrene, just as the Municipal Guard were closing in. But it was sheer devotion that would sustain their bond when they were out in the scrubland, with enemies on all sides. Choosing the most isolated farm for reasons of discretion and prudence, Ferrinho came calling at Three Rivers. Carmina opened the gate to him, wordlessly. He saw her dark eyes and her straight, even teeth, and felt his tough bandit heart unwrap itself. He knew he'd pay for her horse, pay double if she'd asked, a marked departure from his usual business style. She didn't ask a *conto* more, in the end, than the beast was worth.

The dappled mare that Carmina had broken herself, stamped and flinched her ears as the buyer checked her over. But Ferrinho did not look at Carmina, nor she at him. She'd allowed herself a momentary glance when he first showed up, noting his neat suit and wire-framed spectacles from which no one would guess he spent his days in the saddle and nights in the dusty shelter of orchards. He paid her in silver *contos* and she wanted to clasp his hand with the coins in it and never let him go. As he rode off on her fine grey horse, Carmina Bonita watched from the gate, a tight knot of yearning in her chest.

Ferrinho, for days to come, no matter the miles he put between himself and the farm, could not shake the memory of her face.

Within a week she had found him. She kissed her *Mamãe*, and made a last round to feed the animals. She packed a few dresses, her Dermabem liniment and a pistol. With nothing but a hunch to guide her, she rode north on the track to Porto da Folha, but in her rise-and-fall rhythm in the saddle, she reasoned the hunch into pure logic. There were many big farms in the region, wealthy households worth a visit for a young man on the make like Ferrinho. To the south and west lay the shrivelled heart of the *sertão*, the dry, rugged hinterland where only goats endured. And steadily, stealthily, she gained on him.

In the field hemmed with old trees, she dismounted, giddy and terrified. The grey mare she'd sold a week before, tethered in the far corner, sensed her, whinnied in recognition. Behind the mare's flank, a stirring of branches. Carmina froze, standing on the margin of the pasture, the breath of her own horse warm on her shoulder. After a moment she smoothed her skirt, tied her horse to the fence and walked slowly to the centre of the field. Ferrinho, too, broke cover and stood in front of his camp, waiting. He tucked his gun inside his waistband, watching her walk to him as if he'd been expecting her.

When she stood five yards away, he came to face her and looked into her eyes, darker than ever now for being so full of solemnity. When he lunged for her, and threw his arms around her and held her so tight she thought she might never take in air again, it was what he wanted, and it was all that she wanted, and nothing mattered.

In the morning, she browsed the edge of the camp, awkward, while he shaved. She groomed the horses for something to do before he sent her away. He made thick coffee and fried eggs in an iron pan, beckoning her to sit with him and from that moment, Carmina roamed with him and rode with him — all over the *sertão*. Sometimes she'd ride alongside him, sometimes behind on the same saddle. In certain seasons they were joined by members of his band, other times they rode alone. Some days she waited at the camp with the dogs, hoping not to hear gunshots. Now and then she rode with them to the very threshold of a grand house, the feeling of ants creeping up her neck as she waited in the shadows for the moment of confrontation. She cleaned and oiled the pistols for him and set a fire at night when they had outsmarted the police and all the armed men of the estates. But most of all she loved to listen to his low, even voice, as the campfire flashed in his eyes, reciting, like a sacred litany, the wrongs done against his family and the wicked acts of the police. She listened as she would to her grandmother's songs to the roll call of those who'd betrayed the da Silvas, each name chewed over, enunciated with patient malice that verged on tenderness. He had a further list of those 'amigos' on whom he intended to call to request a contribution to the cause. The quiet rhythm of his talk led her into deep sleep, assured of what was right, ever more devoted to her calling and her Ferrinho.

When the police injured one of the men, she would treat the wounds.

"Go see the Captain's woman," the men said. The *Capitão* himself came back in need of her nursing on occasion. Sometimes when she woke in the night, the embers all but dead, the sky bristling with stars, she thought back to her old life. Leaving the farm, *Mamãe* gave her blessing, and when Carmina voiced qualms for her husband, left behind in Santa Brigida with his cobbler's shop, her mother hushed her.

"Forget the old crow, he's too bitter and quick with his fists for you, *filha*."

Mamãe's eyes glittered with the possibilities of escape for Carmina from the pinched life, scratched from dust that awaited her and every other backlands soul.

Once, while recuperating from a heavy battle in an abandoned farmhouse, newspaper reports and local rumour said Ferrinho and his men had raped the girls of the Água Preta plantation when they ransacked the homestead. Carmina flew at him, like a spitting, scratching wildcat. He stood motionless, absorbing her attacks, her fists made strong with rage.

As the others tried to restrain her, he repeated, "*Amor*, it's lies. You know they print lies."

And when she was spent, he sat with her and took her wrists. "Woman, look at me."

She would not.

He spoke anyway. "You know who owns the *Jornal de Pernambuco*?"

125

She craned her head away, looking at nothing but the black ground.

"Anselmo Boa Morte. And you'll know who's his cousin? Governor Coimbra, head of that stinking clan who want my head for a cannonball. If I was Saint Francis of Assisi, they would never write it."

As summer wore on, Carmina spent two nights alone with her belly pressed to the thorny floor of the *caatinga*, her pistol held ready, the sound of her own rapid breathing in her ears. Ferrinho sent her to take cover. Police had poured into the neighbourhood in search of him — flying squads sent by a new governor, eager to win favour with landowners. She lay in waiting, scuttled over by lizards as if she were just another stone. The rocky plain and all the strata beneath seemed to jump with each shot she heard, like beans on a table, dancing to the beat of Easter parade drummers. The reverberations pulsed through her bones.

The men came limping back, with ragged faces and running wounds, to find her. Ferrinho had a bullet wound in his side — chipping the front of his shoulder and grazing his ribs. She knew it was miraculous that the bullet missed his heart but the frail look of him chilled her. They'd have to find somewhere to lie low.

"Where's Marcelinho?" she asked, pressing her neckerchief to his wound, "and your brother?"

He wouldn't answer. She woke in the small hours to find him gone. Most of the others were still asleep nearby, some groaning from their wounds. She lay awake, watching the sky redden like a rage through thorny branches. At dawn, he returned with a sack on his back. He hefted the load further into the scrub, despite his injury. She followed him, but he sent her away. Even from a distance she knew it was not pumpkins in the sack. The noise of his stilted digging, then cursing and digging some more continued, until the heads of Marcelinho and the other fallen comrades were buried.

He emerged from the scrub, his forehead smeared with dried blood, hands caked in earth. "They won't have the pleasure of naming our dead."

The band climbed into the mountains beyond Aurora, far from the flying squads, to find shelter. With altitude came clarity. Carmina realised her idea of Ferrinho as invincible was fantasy. He could be dead within weeks — a septic wound, a police ambush, a betrayal. What would she be then, The Captain's Widow? To the police, The Captain's Whore, for sure. Perhaps one of the other men would take her on as an act of mercy, a loyal shouldering of duty. But how long until the next one was killed? And then, how long until she was seen as some kind of curse, a liability? She could go back to Three Rivers, live out her years a parochial ranch-woman, tending cattle, nursing her mother in her decline, ruminating on the weather. But she'd stood apart from the ordinary folks back home, run off with an outlaw, made herself different. They'd never forget it, not even if she farmed five more decades 'til her back hunched, praying every evening for forgiveness to São Judas, Patron of Lost Causes. As the air grew thinner, she knew that there was only one thing for her to do. He might be killed very soon and the police would put his head on a pole. But better to go out in a blaze with him, beyond the lines that bounded most people's lives, drawing the glare of publicity to the police and their indiscriminate bullets. Better that than crawl off into the *sertão*, like a wounded animal hiding under a rock. She stole glances at him as they

127

reached a scrubby plateau — his steps were faltering, he was becoming feverish.

They neared the ranch of Perereca, whose hatred of the new governor made him an ally of Ferrinho.

The old man met them white-faced, trembling. "Is it really you, *filho*? They said you were dead."

He brought the newspaper, *"BANDIDO MORTO"*. The headless corpse pictured could, from a distance, have been Ferrinho, as much as it could have been anyone.

That night she seized her chance. "It's fate. When people believe something strong enough..." He looked at her, sleepily. "...they won't see the truth even when it's in their face. We can live our life now — a house some place, a few horses, perhaps. No one's going to look for a dead man."

And he smiled strangely at her and fell asleep, clammy and fitful, wrestling the fever. The next night, the same way, she spoke of escape to the quiet life. He nodded and laid his head in her lap, weak as a newborn calf. She cooled him with wet tarpaulin strips. The ring he'd had made for her glimmered in the moonlight — gold from another woman's house smelted into her shape.

Morning lanced through the mountains. He seemed stronger and rose to eat. The men were talking of future campaigns, night strikes on northern towns. As usual Ferrinho raised the stakes, proposing bolder, more daring tactics. She reminded him of his purported death, their chance for a little house, the field with horses.

He looked at her, bemused, trying to fathom the dark tides of her eyes. "Police in three states will thank God for the miracle that Ferrinho's back from the dead," he told the men. "Hell, they'll look fools."

They laughed defiantly. His brother gone, his avenging energy refuelled, there was no persuading him of the peaceful life, the virtues of obscurity. Quietly, with sad determination, she locked away that plan, and pledged herself instead to the path he wanted, the one she had chosen when she chose him.

REMEDIES

"Down, you little mongrel! Sweet Jesus forgive me but I'll kill you." Dona Auxiliadora waves a stick at a small tawny monkey in the boughs of the tree. He has been plucking fruits then dropping them with only one bite gone, and now runs chattering down the trunk to hide in a corner.

"If you're going to eat, eat them, but don't waste them." She waves her stick again, towards the house where the monkey hunches, looking persecuted and small in the damp crevice where the walls meet. "God protect me and guard me!" She shakes her head, walking back to her visitor. "*Hein, hein*, Senhor Prudente, a whole forest around us and he has to pick my jaboticaba fruit to throw on the floor."

Senhor Prudente shakes his head. "Beasts will be beasts," he says, philosophically.

"Now, this trapped wind your wife has been suffering with, is it a night pain she gets or through the day?"

Dona Auxiliadora shows Senhor Prudente around the garden, slowing periodically between questions to run her hand over the bark of a tree, or tug at strap-like leaves sprouting from the soil. Now and then they pause to notice a bird, or despair at the state of local politics. Finally Auxiliadora picks some leaves from a low-growing shrub, wraps them in paper and string and sends Senhor Prudente on his way with instructions on how to make an infusion for his wife. He clasps her hands at the garden gate, telling her how he is indebted to her, that she is

130

nothing short of a saint. The diminutive healer then returns to her yam patch, picks up a hoe, and begins chipping deftly at nut sedge sprouting between the fat yam leaves. After a while, Pinga comes creeping out from his sulking place to help, pulling up the pernicious sedge roots with his long skinny fingers.

"Hnn, you're good for some things, I see. Next time I'll sell you to the Indians and they'll throw you to the alligator," Dona Auxiliadora says, by way of reconciliation.

Far downriver, as Auxiliadora swings her hoe, a journey is beginning. A traveller, gravely afflicted, is starting out up the river in search of healing. In time, the water will bring him to her.

Like the figurehead of a ship, Joelma arrives at the village, sitting ramrod straight in the prow of the motor canoe, silhouetted against golden reflections of late afternoon sky. As her brother-in-law brings the canoe alongside the bank, Joelma scoops up her baggage, and elegantly steps onto the abrupt little beach. Women around the village have heard the boat approach and peep out over washing lines and windowsills to see what she is carrying. They hear her stop first outside Mariela's place, clapping her hands at a polite distance from the front wall, ignoring the little scarecrow of a dog that yips and leaps at the foot of the gate. Soon, Joelma has kissed Mariela goodbye and heads up the track to Auxiliadora's place. Pinga by now is sitting up on the garden wall as if on a lookout post, his tail curling around his feet. He runs yammering to warn Dona Auxiliadora of Joelma's approach. But she is already aware, and eagerly anticipating the sound of palms clapping outside her garden.

And all this time, Auxiliadora knows that the river, snaking towards her in the fading light, bears another passenger, pale and in need of potent remedies.

The women greet each other warmly. Dona Auxiliadora brings water for Joelma to drink, for the sinking sun has lost none of its fire. They catch up on family news, taking a short turn around the herbs and trees that screen the front terrace, with Pinga leaping about in the branches, keeping slightly behind the women. And in the end, slowly and nonchalantly, they return to where they had started.

Joelma tilts one ear to her shoulder. "So..." She holds her empty glass out.

Auxiliadora takes the glass. "So, what have you brought your old friend this month?"

Joelma roots in her capacious shoulder bag that's printed all over with tiny Brahma beer logos. "Well, Dona Dora, there's your Contessa de Montefiori nail polish. Then..."

Auxiliadora takes the dark little vial and looks down at her toes, damp and specked with soil.

"About time," she says, slipping one foot out of its sandal. "I'm walking around like this with no pedicure for three weeks. Imagine!"

"Ah, well now you'll be restored to your usual beauty, won't you? And then there's your order of Creme de Rosas."

Dona Auxiliadora smiles, stretching out her arms to receive the pots of cream.

"And Senhor Aécio's cologne." Joelma pulls out a glass bottle with a picture of a yacht on the label. Auxiliadora regards the yacht and thinks of the ailing traveller, lying still and watchful on the puttering boat, moving nearer to her, his chest swelling with hope.

"How is the Senhor?" asks Joelma.

"Oh, God willing he'll be home with us for Lent. He is weakened a little now, he needs to be in his own bed."

"*Querida*, if anything's going to give him strength it's being here with the folks he loves." Joelma squeezes Auxiliadora's forearm. "You give him a big hug from me now."

"I will." She goes indoors to get her purse. Coming back out she asks, "Now how did that compress work out for your Moizé?"

"He's breathin' much easier, thanks to you, Dora." Joelma slaps at a mosquito on her smooth brown shoulder. "He still has a bit of a hacking cough — just a little irritation though."

"Uh-huh? Well now let me take a look at my hyssop bushes. I wonder did they recover from the weevil that got them..."

The women walk towards a circle of bushy herbs in the direction of the gate.

"Not bad — they are looking stronger." Auxiliadora picks a handful of hyssop sprigs for Joelma. "Tell him to draw a basin of hot water, steep a spoonful of these in it. Then, drape a towel over his head like a curtain and inhale the steam."

"God bless you, Dona Dora." Joelma embraces her and turns towards the gate.

"Twice a day for a week, it will loosen the cough." Auxiliadora watches her go, then takes her cosmetics into the kitchen.

In a hammock on the terrace, Auxiliadora files and polishes her toes and rubs Creme de Rosas into her feet by the light of the lamp over the kitchen door. Pinga grabs at moths attracted to the electric glow. He studies the twitching captives clutched like fat and succulent palm nuts, cocking his head to one side and the other, occasionally nibbling them like exotic delicacies.

Auxiliadora thinks of her Aécio when he was strong and broad, and begins to sing the song that he used to sing for her.

'O, gardener girl
Why do you look so sad?
What could it be that has befallen you?
Was it the camellia
That fell from the branch
Gave two sighs from the heart
Then withered up and died?'

He is coming soon, coming home for her to heal him. Pinga lifts his gaze from his fingers, silvered with moth dust, and listens to the melancholy singing.

'Come, gardener girl,
Come, O my love.
Don't be sad
'Cause this world
Is all yours,
You are much more beautiful
Than the camellia that died.'

It is an old, old song. Auxiliadora's dark eyes are shining with tears. Daví will come in the morning for another love cure. And after him, perhaps Dona Carmim will be back with her leg ulcer, needing a fresh poultice. But soon they are bringing home her Aécio, who used to sing to her, whose arms were once so bunched up with muscles, whose labour provided for them all those years. He is near now, and full of hope. Aéçio, love of her life, all shrunken and weak. They are bringing him up the river on the ambulance boat, from the hospital where they have tried all their cures, used them all up. There is nothing left now but to find him comfort in the familiar nooks and corners of home, with the garden scents drifting through the window. And stinging, bitter tears spill over her cheeks, for though the camellias grow tall and strong as she prunes and feeds them, in the whole of her garden there is nothing that can help him.

SWEET VICTORY

She dreaded the burning season, the cane-cutter's daughter. Each year when the cane was ripe, its tough leaves set ablaze before cutting, flames conjured her Papai — out of the very smoke that killed him. In smouldering cane-fields, she pressed her hands over her ears, but his cinder-toffee breaths slithered between her fingers. "This work gonna ruin your lungs, *querida*." She picked up her machete and swung at charred sugarcanes, cursing.

The year before, in desperation, she'd started running to escape her daddy's soot-faced visitations. After each day's cutting, she traded ashen overalls for shorts, and sprinted between stubbly fields stitched through with still-winking embers. Reaching green swathes of unburned cane, she'd ease up, feel her chest expand. Rustling cane-chapels overhead and her heart hammering at her ribs finally muffled Papai's dire warnings.

The Sugar Plantation proudly sponsored a team for the famous São Silvestre Race; four muscled men running for glory, and her, fleeing her daddy's ghost. Race-day, Papai tailed her all the way to the big city on the bus, wheezing in her ear, "Cane-smoke gonna kill you too, my angel."

As the plantation bus prowled the suburbs she pictured his brow rumpled with worry. Behind the start-line, she pinned a number on her chest, determined to outrun his scorched shadow. BANG! The starter-gun jolted her daddy's breaths into rhythmic, rasping gasps, always just behind her. On baking asphalt between mirrored offices, she built up speed. "Faster, further," her athlete's soul demanded. "Cannot, cannot!" pleaded her legs and lungs. And in her mind, the spectators lining the streets were whispering cane-rows under a wide blue sky.

Her chest pressed against the finish-ribbon, ticker tape cascaded from skyscrapers. She saw the crowds' wide-open mouths, cheering, though all she could hear was her own deafening pulse.

Nine hot miles turned her into an athlete with champion lungs, anticipating life without sugar-soot. She raised her medal in calloused cane-cutting hands, to ecstatic roars. Her eyes welled, her athlete's heart, strong and healthy, ached with joy. And Papai? Papai was silent with pride. From the corner of her eye she saw a twist of cane soot falling, a wisp fading against the sun.

The Last Puppeteer

Zé da Viola was disconsolate. Unemployed and disconsolate. He'd become unemployed at the word of the plantation foreman, the man's thick-lined face carefully washed of sympathy — of any feeling at all. It was a simple message, a factual communication conveyed in a business-like manner. Tears and emotional displays were a waste of liquid and energy in these drought-harrowed parts. There had been work, yesterday and for years before, and now there was none.

The tall cane watched Zé as he walked among the furrows where he had cut and planted and hoed for so many seasons. The sugarcane whispered to him, "Why are you still here?" In the distance he heard the trucks and noise of the other cutters at work and knew he was no longer one of them. It seemed strange, this dismissal out of the blue, but he knew better than to ask questions. His hands, shined and cracked like shoe leather, were not needed for cutting here. He did not belong to this field, to this earth, fat and silvered with sugar roots.

The old mare watched Zé returning to his shack on the plantation margins. She sensed, with her twitching tail and ears, some change. He looked around at his possessions. They were few: a chipped table, his radio and guitar, a couple of pans, enamelled plates and cups, a shirt or two, and on the wall a football pennant and São Judas, patron saint of lost causes, his hammock, bedding, the fridge that needed painting. He'd never felt the lack of more furniture, of fancy shoes or gadgets. These things had always been enough, while he worked. A man who had work had his riches in the fibres of his own arms. He could buy rice, beans, a little cane liquor for the end of the day — he didn't need a lot more. If a man had work.

He stepped out for a moment to look down on the plantation, his fingers untying knots in the mare's mane. The acres where he had cut cane for years stretched to the horizon, the processing plant the only landmark, its striped stack topped with a twist of pale, sticky smoke. The workers moved like tiny beetles on the red roads between fields, although mostly they were hidden inside the sea of silver, waving cane. From his pocket, Zé took the few dampened notes given by the foreman. He spread them on the bed, pinning his gaze on them as if trying to discern his future among their watermarks and famous faces.

When he woke it was already dawn. Sun combed pink waves through the cane fields. Time to go cutting, for everyone except Zé. He sat, resting his face in his hands. Ants made a column along the doorjamb and the mare stamped the ground, hungry. The mare's impatience, the ants' industry, provoked a shudder, a sudden rush of urgency. The need to find work, the knowledge that it wouldn't be easy — he knew nothing else but cane cutting. Out of nowhere, a fleeting memory came to him. Standing, slowly, he reached to the shelf above the bed, lifted down a wooden box. Inside, laid head to toe, piled one upon the other, were a cast of puppets, a little stage-weary, their painted eyes still vivid, their names and characters alive in his mind.

The puppets were musty-smelling, moulting, their clothes worn into brittle folds by the years spent entombed in layers. Underneath them, lay the posts and chintz curtains that made the theatre booth. A spider, flattened inside the lid, had died waiting for the next show. The familiar characters lifted in turn from the box rekindled Zé's best memories of his father. The old man had been rough-tempered. Often drunk, he spoke crudely to Zé's mother and was too worn out with work to have much to do with the kids. But now and then he took down the Mamulengo theatre box and played for Zé and the other kids and locals, and he was transformed. The gruff, distant father became proud puppet-master: animated, knowledgeable, admired, in control of his puppets and their destinies, in charge of happy endings.

Afterwards, he'd show Zé how to carve a new head, to mend a hand with a tiny shaving of wood, to manipulate the rods that made puppets dance, drink and fight. "Pay attention, José," he always said, "there's not many know how to work these puppets any more."

Little Zé watched and learned from his father and wanted to be him. Watching the show, hearing his father sing and play guitar, he was lost in a world where good won out, women were beautiful and beloved and men were brave, a place where the lowly worker triumphed over greedy planters and the rain came when people wished hard enough and crops grew strong.

Leading his horse between the whispering fields, Zé didn't look back. The mare was loaded with bedding and shirts, his radio and his São Judas. Tied level across her rump was the puppet box, wrapped in a sheet.

Novo Mundo bore the signs of being another squalid little knot of liquor and grain stores serving local ranches. Road-signs were leprous with bullet holes, the handiwork of ranch-hands on their way home, made brave and belligerent with cane brandy. Zé crossed the municipal boundary at noon, expecting to leave the place behind him in a quarter mile. But he rode another hour before the centre. Neat houses strung along the roadside with laundry pegged out and dogs minding the yard. The town square, when he finally reached it, was a kaleidoscope of busy market stalls, bound by a town hall, shops, bars, barbeque joints and a church. Beyond the stalls, the square opened into a sandy expanse shaded by jatobá trees, and dotted with benches. The theatre would fit well there, with room for plenty of spectators.

In a bar off the main drag, Zé ordered cane brandy, the first of many, and tried not to think about how he'd pay. He began playing his guitar and passed the hours like that, drinking, singing, playing and drinking. The talk in the place was of the drought, farmers packing up and heading south, and of the latest political corruption scandal. By the bar, the owner held forth on the rot at the heart of government, unblocking saltshakers with a toothpick that he also used to skewer the air and gesture at the newspaper as he made his points.

"The politicians promised the earth before the elections. And now? Where were they now?" The barman shook his head, waltzing between the tables with beer mats.

Before the sun fully set, and before Zé was quite incoherent, a guy with a beard showed up, carrying a drum. Eyeing Zé suspiciously, he sat by the door. Zé set down his guitar and nodded, hoping he'd play. The drum remained untouched. Another drink downed, Zé's impatience piqued and his inhibitions loosened, he strode over and asked the drummer to strike up some rhythms.

141

Rangel was his name. He turned slowly to Zé and motioned at the guitar abandoned on the bar. It turned out they both knew the usual tunes, some folk songs, the familiar samba anthems. They played together a while, then Zé let the drummer play while he observed, watching to see if his hands had the necessary agility. He was a little serious, didn't show much sense of humour, but he played well enough. Rangel signed up as accompanist for the first show.

Zé watered the horse and sat in the shade working on his puppets. Rangel came to rehearse with him, out by the railway. He listened to the plot, a simple tale of Zé's own invention, the cane-cutter thrusting puppets forwards as their characters stepped into the limelight. Zé gave the minor roles to Rangel, hoping his quick drummer's hands could turn from drum skin to puppet rods in a second, and that his sense of rhythm would twist and jiggle characters into life on cue. The drummer worked out some riffs to cinch people's ribs with tension, a pounding, hostile signature for the villain, and for the finale, a *frevo*, defiantly joyous, though Rangel remained pokerfaced. Zé felt himself a little clumsy in working the puppets, but figured he could distract from awkward moments with his strong voice, speaking the fears and secret hopes of characters as if from their very hearts of wood, just as his father did. They put up signs around town, written on scraps of cardboard, advertising the '*ESPETÁCULO*' to come that night.

In timid groups, people walked by, shooting curious glances towards the wooden frame and coloured curtains under the jatobá trees. The puppeteers nodded and beckoned, playing soft melodies, but no one sat. Around the bars they went with drum and guitar. A modest band of men, far from sober, and a few couples, followed them back to the puppet booth. A few more folk just coming out of church were swept up in the crowd.

A very old man, all bent over, remarked, "Mamulengo puppets! Haven't seen those since the days when we used gas lights."

Eventually, with an audience of nineteen and two dogs, the show began.

Spurred by hunger and nerves, Zé played a frenetic opening *maracatú*, Rangel struggled to keep up. The first scene opened well, João, poor but hard-working ranch-hand, and Marilene his sweetheart, won applause, while Damião, ranch foreman, full of lust for Marilene and ill-will towards João, drew unequivocal hissing. The spectators shouted to warn João as traps were set for him and yelled as Damião plotted to send him away, leaving Marilene alone, vulnerable to the foreman's whim. Zé had his characters feign deafness now and then to provoke louder shouts. Rangel's nervous farm-boy made the crowd laugh, serenading Marilene to seduce her for Damião, and being mistaken in the dark for her beloved João. The prim falsetto Zé affected for Marilene's lines broke down into a croak here and there. The crowd resorted to giggles. Delays between setting down the guitar and picking up the puppet rods slackened the pace. Sweating, Zé threw all his energies towards the final showdown between João and his exploitative boss. Rangel's heavy, hypnotic beat built tension and the night air was taut like a guitar string.

Zé peered through the chintz curtains at the spectators, sunken-cheeked, blank-eyed people, scrawny and desiccated, like strips of sun-jerked beef. The vigour had been drained out of them, evaporated by drought, their energy and drive stolen by years without rain and trampled by an endless carnival of corrupt politicians. Shiny promises and free tee-shirts in election season were dependably followed in the spring by raids on the municipal coffers, leaving hospitals without medication, schools without books, dams and reservoirs still unfinished.

Rocking the rods back and forth, Zé brought João to his feet resurrected by his sweetheart's singing. Lunging towards the audience, the lustful foreman made one last attack on his rival, but João's strength was immense now, spurred on by Marilene's devotion. Damião knocked to the floor, the happy couple danced a great ruckus. Rangel drummed frantically and Zé reached down to pick out a few chords on his guitar, laid on the ground, all the while spinning the lovers in a wild jig.

But the audience had seen so many stories like this — good guy fights bad guy and gets the girl. The same plot danced through these streets in countless different ways at festival time, with inventive costumes and music. Zé's version, played straight along the old lines, was routine as rice and beans. No surprises or twists. Whether they foresaw the ending and were bored, or just didn't believe in it, they were not roused, no matter how hard Rangel drummed and Zé stomped his foot and put his heart into the song. A frail applause followed the curtain and five of the nineteen drifted away before the collection hat had begun its round. The benches emptied and the battered hat, hastily returned to the front, contained two bottle tops, a button, a crumpled prayer to Santo Expedito and thirty *centavos*.

The puppeteers didn't say much to each other. Zé was disappointed in himself, thought he'd be more of a natural.

"It's a lot to manage, puppets, voices and music..." he said, a little envious of the laughs Rangel got for his nervous farm-boy.

"Yup." Rangel shrugged in agreement.

They'd have to do better if they were going to earn enough to get by.

The two ordered workmen's dinners in a bar. The takings were not quite enough to get roaring drunk. They ate in silence. Three old men by the door were arguing over the lead story of the People's Gazette, a scandal centring on Magro, the catering magnate, supplier to schools and hospitals across Brazil of hot meals served in foil dishes. Magro was accused of mixing in animal slops.

"They're calling this Magro joker 'The Marmitex King,'" the most grizzled of the three gents read aloud, turning towards the bar. "Even street dogs turn their noses up at his Marmitex meals."

The bartender wafted a dismissive hand toward the newspaper. "Let's see how long before he bribes his way out of trouble."

The three old men continued their disagreement about the source of the rancid food. Zé watched them — so animated, indignant fingers stubbed into the table. He imagined the curtain rising on the Marmitex King, a smug and loathsome villain, the three old boys roaring their revulsion, shaking their fists. But the real puppet masters, roaming the *sertão*, stuck to traditional plots, honed over generations, full of suspense and melancholy, tension and laughs. Magro was just a fat guy in a suit, and Zé, bruised by his first adventure in storytelling, thought he'd be safer

145

staying with the time-honoured stories that worked for the old *mamulengeiros*. A peppered breeze got up, dredging red dust across the square. A violet haze filled the doorway as sun set on Novo Mundo.

The barman switched on the television for the game and the place filled up. Two women in tight jeans and brash make-up patiently nursed long drinks, waiting for lulls in the football when men's attention came around to them again. During the first half, a new arrival caught the women's curiosity. Tall and fair, he pulled up a stool, heaving a bulky lacquered case to the floor, and began doing card tricks. Zé eyed the case: accordion-shaped. At half time a small crowd gathered. The tricks grew more elaborate. The audience shook their heads, bewildered by the cards' impossible migrations and the treachery of their own eyes. Surrounded by new friends, the tall guy ordered a beer as the second half began.

Motioning towards the instrument case, Zé asked, "D'you play?"

After the game, the trickster switched cards for accordion and filled the place with music. His playing was decent, and his charisma could revive the Mamulengo shows. Rangel said nothing. The accordionist was a builder, but said work had dried up lately, like the rain. Drought got people thinking of leaving rather than building. Zé's terms were stark: no payment unless he livened up the audiences and boosted takings. It was good enough for a jobless builder.

The card sharp said his name was Dorival. A tiny flinch of his eye, not quite a wink, left Zé wondering if this was his name, and if not, what he was hiding.

For the next show, Zé had been thinking of 'Captain' Lampião and Maria Bonita, the sweetheart bandits in half-moon hats. They might strike a chord with the dried up, disappointed people of the backlands, with their long history of being cheated and trampled on. The bandits, so he told the two musicians, were the underdogs who bit back, the poor people's champions standing up against lawless Sugar Colonels and the corrupt National Guard. This could be the story to get through the leathery skins of these people, to whisk their blood, nudge their hearts, uncork their tears. He could make the outlaws from his father's puppets. All he needed were half-moon hats and Lampião's trademark spectacles, looped from a scrap of wire. Pedra Rosa, the next town on the road to the interior, was bigger than Novo Mundo, according to local opinion, and closer to the heartland of the original bandit saga.

"We might find descendants of Lampião himself," said Zé. "Who knows, they may pay well for our tribute to their outlaw ancestor."

Rangel shrugged. Dorival pursed his lips thoughtfully and swung the accordion on his back.

On the thorn-edged road, they heard the plan for the show. The accordionist's thick countryside accent was not helped by the lisp that whistled when his tongue pressed air over the empty stretch of gum between his canines. Zé kept the speaking parts for himself and Rangel, though the drummer had become all but mute — roughly since Dorival arrived. Dust rose in sheets from the parched fields along the roadside, coating men and horses in a dull terracotta. Soon the three looked like the clay figurines bought by tourists on the way north to Amazonas.

An ancient cashew marked the city boundary. It had retained most of its leaves, even in these dried up times — a landmark among shadeless acres of scrub. They tied up the horses. Rangel went ahead to find a good spot for the show. Dorival sat on an upturned oilcan and picked out some syncopated sequences for Lampião's gun battles and some nimble chase themes for bandits fleeing to mountain hideouts. Nodding approval, Zé listened, his hands at work bending new wire spectacles over the ears of the bandit Lampião. They made him look menacing, perhaps because they lent an air of intellect turned towards brutal ends. Next, he pulled the bandit's companion from the puppet chest. Dorival said nothing, but his eyes slid towards the cashew roots beneath his boots.

"Here's the *bandida* — not bad for a girl squashed up in a box for thirty years, eh?" Zé's upbeat tone was unconvincing.

The accordionist made a non-committal grunt, his fingers slowing on the keys.

"What's the problem?" Zé shook the puppet as if the indignation was hers.

Dorival shrugged awkwardly under the straps of the instrument. "Maria Bonita... she's not so *bonita.*"

And he put the accordion down and went over into the scrub to pee.

The puppet's face was scratched, her eyes lopsided. Her red-painted lips had suffered a large chip, giving her the unfortunate appearance of a backlands girl with half her teeth missing. The cruellest effect of Maria's years in mothballs was hair loss. The tufts that remained were brittle and dull, sprouting at stubborn angles from her wooden scalp. Even in Zé's affectionate gaze, she was a fright. Toothless, balding, it was not how people imagined the daring heroine they nicknamed Bonita.

In silence, Zé stood and set off on the road to town. Dorival squeezed a melancholy tune, watching him shrink against the reddening horizon. At the door of a gabled house, Zé took off his hat. A woman greeted him, her Afro hair bound in coloured cloth, greying flashes at her temples, full lips painted deep red. Inside, girls lounged on sofas or leant against a counter between bottles of *cashaça*, a telephone, a vase of plastic roses. They poured drinks. One sat in his lap, another fooled around wearing his hat. But the one he wanted was at the counter, her glorious black hair shimmering down her back. When they were alone in the room and she unzipped her dress, he thought of nothing else but the ample curves of her buttocks and filled his hands with warm, firm flesh. Her black eyes watched him, almost curious. Afterwards, pulling on his dusty clothes, he hesitated to open his wallet.

"Your hair is beautiful."

Her face hardened. She moved over, kneading his shoulders in an impatient rhythm.

"Can I have a lock...as a keepsake?"

He turned to face her, her expression impervious, save for a slight crease appearing briefly between her eyebrows. She left the room. Zé waited. He expected shouting, the turbanned woman to show him the door. The girl returned with scissors. She lifted her curtain of hair leaving a few strands loose at the neck.

"No more than a finger's-length." She turned her back. "I should charge you extra."

Maria Bonita's puppet was transformed with her glossy cane-black hair. The company set up the little theatre tent next to a bar. Customers wouldn't have to leave their drinks to watch, and, loosened up by alcohol, may part more easily with their coins. Dorival warmed up the crowd with popular melodies and soon people were requesting tunes. Zé tuned his guitar and lined up the puppets: police, bandits and Sugar Colonels. They opened to a crowd of over fifty. The accordion music made the show somehow bigger, more alive. The audience howled in despair when Lampião was ambushed. Maria Bonita's sassy lines drew whoops of appreciation. The gun battles were electric: disjointed wheezes of the accordion and explosive popping sounds from Rangel's mouth — bullets whistling through scrubby valleys. But somewhere around half way, both Zé and the audience realised that the story was going to end in betrayal as it always did, with the bandits' heads on poles and the police victorious. Police and the politicians always got away with it in real life. Who wanted to watch the same thing happen in a theatre show? The people had fallen silent, one or two jeered. The first egg hit the back of the puppet booth. The second barely missed Rangel's left ear. A sulphurous reek drove the puppeteers from the booth and the crowd from their bar tables.

Things looked clearer now in the mirror surface of his cane brandy. Hunched over his glass, Zé saw his eyes reflected in the liquor: they were not artist's eyes. In his father's day, the whole street filled with crowds pushing in to see the puppets. People climbed on lampposts and roofs, dancing, shouting at the stage. But that was then. Now everyone had TV and nobody cared about stories of long-dead bandits. There was no escape from sugar cane — he'd fooled himself for a while, but like every other sucker round here, he'd have to go to the plantations in the morning and see who was hiring.

Some hours later, Rangel slunk into the bar.

"Lampião's no use." Zé made a swatting gesture. "Who wants to see a guy rise up then get killed by police?"

The drummer shook his head, waving to the barman to bring another glass.

Zé continued, "A psychopath. The police, sure, they're rotten to the core, but Lampião went round murdering and raping, no better than them. Nobody round here remembers him anyway."

Rangel picked at calluses on his drumming hand. "People like rebels who stand up against the authorities. It just needs a better ending."

Swirling the dregs in his glass, Zé tutted. "It's like my father said, nobody knows Mamulengo any more, it's a lost art. It won't be some peasant like me who brings it back to life. I'm good for cutting cane, that's all. Forget it man, go home."

Rangel spat in the dust. His eyes had a dark glitter. "You ignorant bastard. This thing can make a living for two, three men if you work at it."

Zé scowled, his bloodshot eyes looking devilish. "What d'you know? Never set eyes on a puppet theatre before last month, now you're the expert? Drummers like you are glad to run alongside the Carnaval parade with the street dogs."

Rangel staggered to his feet, swaying, "Zé da Viola, eh?" He swung at Zé, hitting his cheekbone with a satisfying crack. "Loser can't string three chords together."

Reeling in his chair, Zé's hand flew up to his face. He pushed himself up from the table, the shot glass rolling in diminishing arcs, his red eyes slowly levelling on Rangel. He leant back, rounding his arm ready to shut the percussionist up, but the barman grabbed him from behind and shoved both men out into the square.

Morning sun sifted through the broad leaves of the cashew tree, warming Zé's face. Grit pressed against his cheek. He found he could open only one eye, the other was tender and fat like raw mignon. His head throbbed noisily; he decided not to move. The light was too strong on his eye and he closed it. Something tickled in the crook of his elbow. A column of ants marched from under the cashew roots, over his arm and towards something shiny, a discarded foil package. Squeezing his eye half-shut to focus better, the print on the cellophane wrapper resolved into a familiar logo: 'Magro Marmitex', the 'M's drawn as little crowns.

Now Zé propped himself up on his elbows, dusting the ants from his skin. There in the foil dish were the remnants of a meal and the beginnings of a story that people cared about, the Marmitex Scandal. It had been happening all year, filling the newspapers and TV screens — the big company with contracts to feed half the hospital patients and school kids in the country using slops not fit for pigs to bulk out their meals. It was the story that outraged housewives chatting at the grocer's, riled the old guys drinking *aguardente*, thumping their fists on tin tables in bars. It was another story whose ending everyone knew already — the multi-millionaire Marmitex King would go to court, be condemned and sentenced, but would never serve his term. It was always the way. But this was an ending people couldn't accept — the injustice of it rankled, aching in people's bellies, snagging in their throats. Zé could bring Magro to account in his theatre. People would jump up and hiss and make speeches. He saw how he could create a modern-day Lampião to speak for the people — a hero they could believe in, who would take pot shots at the corrupt and the rich, at ruthless big business, poke fun at politicians. In the world-in-miniature of the Mamulengo theatre, at least, they could bring down the villains of the day. Rangel, arrogant fool that he was, had been right on that score: audiences liked rebels.

Zé stood and brushed grit from his clothes. He mounted his horse and looked around for the musicians. Like the farmers hereabouts whose hopeful sowings were answered each year with drought, he was going to try again.

Sanctuary

Dawn came to the beach, raking bloody streaks through the sky. Bran squinted at the horizon; a smoky pall hung over the city's frayed skyline, though all was quiet. He rose, stretched, rolled his blanket. Up by the beach wall, behind him a little way, the Mute was brewing coffee on a small crackling flame. With some stubborn effort of will he'd revived last night's damp embers. His black hair stood up in uneven combs like a sickly cockatiel. They sipped the strong brew, staring into the coals: one cup, then another. Under the bridge with its crumbling pillars, a boat nodded, its hull half cradled in shingle, roughly tethered to a rotten stump. They slipped the barnacled rope from its mooring and rowed out into the bay, keeping in the bridge's shadow. The water was filmy and the oars sluggish. Egrets, indifferent to the boat's churning, stabbed at unseen prey, picking morsels from the scum with an unthinking rhythm.

Under a strengthening sun, they pulled the boat up on an anonymous muddy spit a quiet distance around the bay from the port. They headed for Tijuca Hill, from where the garrison was thought to command the city. The slums were battered, but the damage unremarkable, their usual appearance of jumbled squalor unaltered. More genteel *bairros* bore their scars with showy pathos — substantial, very public woundings, roofs fallen away leaving exposed beams, truncated pillars and facades acned with bullet holes. Bran kept close to the walls that remained, diverted to alleys where possible to avoid sniper fire, the Mute slinking along in his shadow. They walked all morning through smoking rubble and met barely a soul. A vendor stacked up mangoes for nobody, a hooker smoked *charutos* in a glassless window, an old man with festering leg wounds sat in the shade of a plaster scale-model of Christ the Redeemer, awaiting salvation against the odds.

Twice they came close — too close — to ragged bands of renegade fighters building sandbag barricades, or staking out the roof of an old hotel. The Mute understood immediately Bran's hand signals and ducked back into a doorway, around a corner. They walked a looping route towards the base of Tijuca, striking across the city, detouring to avoid open areas and troop patrols. Nearing the general's camp, they climbed into mist, the Mute following closer now. Guards blocked the road, their chests braced with bandoliers. One of them stepped forward, beckoning Bran, his jaw jerking to one side. Bran spoke low and quiet; the guard fixed his eyes on the horizon. He motioned to Bran to follow but ordered the Mute to stay. They climbed a rutted dirt road through rows of troop tents, the canvas dusty and threadbare. Soldiers smoked in hammocks slung between trees and flagpoles. The Mute hunkered down, dejected, under the jaded gaze of the remaining guard.

Abruptly Bran was thrust towards a young soldier.

"Take him to Ramiros," the Guard said and Bran followed the slender khaki back towards a shelled building. The soldier bowed slightly at an open doorway and left. Bran looked back at the ramshackle camp, then ducked under the sagging lintel to peer inside.

"*Alô?*" Bran clapped his hands, still standing on the threshold. "Senhor General?"

There were soft sounds of nearby movement. A patched tarpaulin hung from the rafters, partitioning the room into smaller chambers. From behind this divider, a tall man appeared, buttoning up his trousers as he strode towards the middle of the floor, plucking a peaked cap from the wall as he moved and shucking it neatly onto his head. He turned to face Bran.

"General Ramiros?" Bran extended his hand.

"The same." The General tightened his belt, eyeing Bran suspiciously.

"I am Bran. I've come to talk with you about a mission of mercy."

The general slowly reached out to shake his hand. A nervous-looking private, clutching his hat, bolted from behind the tarpaulin. His darting exit set the canvas swaying, revealing a bed with rumpled sheets. The General's gaze did not waver.

"What kind of mission?" asked the General.

"It concerns some forgotten inhabitants of this city," Bran said. "Barely surviving in distressing conditions."

"Won't you sit?" The General gestured, impassive, towards a large steel desk in the corner.

The men leant their elbows on opposite sides of the cool metal. Bran went ahead and explained more, knowing there was little point in speaking obliquely with a man who buttoned up his fatigues nonchalantly in front of strangers.

"I came to talk to you about the creatures of this city's zoological park." He waited a moment to allow the General to digest this, and to gauge how best to proceed.

The General's facial muscles did not twitch. His gaze, in the shadow of the peaked brim, fixed steadily on Bran. "Go on."

"The animals are suffering. Some are sick. All are starving. Some have already succumbed. The keepers have enlisted, or taken their families to the countryside. Only one remains, and he's going crazy watching the beasts die, not able to do anything for them."

The General watched him. Bran had no high hopes of this man of war, he did not expect that his face might pucker with emotion over zoo creatures.

"Why did you come to me?" The General laid his arms neatly, one on top of the other on the desk.

"General, only you can help. We can't get feed across the city with the blockade, so I need to take the animals out. Just a couple of hours without exchange of fire. Is it possible?"

The General paced the room, rubbing his moustache. "I used to take my daughter to the zoo. She loved those animals. They used to have a bear....Pata Larga, 'Big Paw'. He was her favourite."

Bran watched, and for a moment began to feel a childish hope, despite himself, a belief in the General's humanity. "Pata Larga is still there. Very weak, but still holding on."

The General stood in the doorway and a runner appeared. Breathlessly, he answered questions from the General, short affirmations and numbers. But Bran was not able to follow most of the exchange. His language wasn't up to it, or his hearing was fading, worn thin by the percussion of too many war zones. The runner had gone, like a pinball pelted down the slope by orders from the man at the top.

"Be ready at three o'clock." The General spoke, still gazing out on his camp. "You will have until nightfall. You will take Maria Pequena with you — that way you'll find the safe routes." He turned to face the man who would rescue Pata Larga.

Bran could think of no reply. He had no words to express the gratitude and relief he felt, without conveying utter disbelief and the low expectations he'd held of the man.

"General, I am most grateful."

Ramiros cut him off with a waved hand. Engine noise came grinding towards the building.

"Take the vehicles, fit them out as you require and return before three. Behind the camp, there is an abandoned farm. You may find straw bales and some fodder."

Bran drove down the hill in an old jeep, his head a bedlam of thoughts. Two more cars flanked him, four military trucks followed. The Mute was squatting under a cashew tree, his attention entirely dedicated to a trail of ants. Not until Bran honked the horn, just three yards away, did he look up and jump aboard, grinning.

They loaded bales and feed sacks at the farm. Soldiers from the other vehicles helped with the work, waiting for Bran to organise them. Unaccustomed to this sudden authority, he spoke in requests rather than orders, over polite, formal, motioning towards the dilapidated barn where he had seen more hay. They seemed to understand him despite his apprentice grammar and the heavy accent. He was distracted, thrown by his complete failure to anticipate the General's behaviour. Bribes, yes, he had been ready for that. A damp roll of banknotes sat where he'd tucked it this morning, snug against the skin of his hipbone. But a ceasefire without bribery, requisitioned vehicles, a whole convoy at his disposition — this he had never imagined. And now he went about stocking the cars with a complex crinkle in his brow, running through all the possible reasons a powerful military man would do these things for a stranger, a gringo. Bran could be setting himself up for the biggest trap yet in all his years of working in cities under siege. But why — the General had enemies enough to focus on; he'd hardly waste time on a lone gringo showing up unannounced.

The soldiers had found a half bottle of cachaça at the farmhouse and were passing it around. One of them looked so slight and gentle, Bran felt a protective pang. Just the hint of moustache, nothing worth wetting a razorblade for, smooth pink cheeks and dark hair, slick under his cap. While the others laughed and joked, he was quiet, though he stood with them, looking out over the scarred cityscape through the copper lens of the cachaça bottle. They came back to Bran eventually to hear what the next operation would be. Back to HQ to await the ceasefire. They scattered to the trucks and jeeps.

"Maria!" A set of keys tossed in a high arc to the smooth-cheeked one. "Take the Mercedes." Gentle-faced conscript, Maria Pequena climbed up into the cab.

Back at the camp, Bran spread a map on the table and located the zoo.

Maria studied the squares of her city with an arched brow and declared, "Maps are close to useless, many bridges have been shelled, some roads are impassable. The best way out will be south to the port at Todos Os Anjos, then inland on the barges, or on the old towpath, with any animals that can walk."

Surreptitiously, the Mute slid out of Bran's jeep and installed himself in the passenger seat of Maria's Mercedes truck. At 14.55 the convoy drove to the camp gate again, and southwest to the zoo.

The map indeed turned out to be more or less irrelevant. At first they seemed to be following the main artery to the south, cratered and deserted as it was. But only a short distance down the trunk route the lead truck veered off onto a minor road. Bran's co-driver explained the next section was a notorious stretch for ambush. Bran felt overwhelmed with sorrow for the stricken city. He'd visited often as a young man and remembered a shimmering, cosmopolitan, sensuous place of confident, friendly people. Now the few residents they saw were hunched and darting for cover or begging amid squalor. They had to backtrack for miles when an expected bridge had been destroyed. Maria Pequena in the vanguard — her sleek bobbed hair uncovered, her sunglasses catching the sun — led the convoy on winding diversions through miserable districts inhabited mainly by vultures.

After a long and dusty drive, the vehicles entered the Zoo Park. The Mute jumped down from the Mercedes, excited like a puppy, gambolling towards the gate. Maria thrust out an arm, pulling him back by the collar.

She spoke sternly to him, gesturing towards shell cases and debris over the path ahead. "These could be live. You have to wait."

The soldiers got to work making a thorough search of the forecourt, then moved in through the gates. Creepers and tall heliconia thrust through the rusted railings, scrambled over the arched sign above the entrance. Dark runnels of mould stained the walls. Bran walked behind the bomb-disposal crew and beckoned the Mute, sat motionless in the truck since Maria's warning. The stink was toxic. Carcasses littered the ground, their ribs arcing into the air, innards brimful of maggots.

The cages had been partially cannibalised for scrap metal, chains and padlocks. Some small birds hunched in a filthy aviary, listless, unblinking. A jaguar, bony like a rusty gate, lay in a heap in the corner of a fetid enclosure. An otter, missing its front paw, lay on concrete by a dried-up pool. A macaw, facing the back wall of its pen, bobbed and bowed in a psychotic, hollow frenzy, its mate dead on the ground, maggots wriggling in her eye. The last jacketed anteater hovered like a wraith, striped by cage-bar shadows, so emaciated and light, she seemed almost to be levitating. The saddest thing was her snout — once eighteen fleshy inches of gently arching, velvety proboscis — perfect for nuzzling spicy insects from cracks in the earth; now a threadbare hook, shrivelled and droopy.

Snakes fared better, their static coils conserved energy longer than the restless, eager mammals and birds. And who knew what opportune snacks they had enjoyed as fellow creatures weakened. Abutting the llama paddock, where at least two black llamas and a small alpaca family could be seen lain out under clouds of flies, was a small partially roofed avian enclosure. Small trees crowded through the wire walls and perches jammed across the width of the pen at various heights and angles. From this shaded corner came a slow sobbing sound. Bran moved towards it. He eased the door open; it ground on the floor, its rusty hinges crunched. Bran advanced, calling softly to whoever might be inside. The sobs were interspersed with low muttering, the muttering in turn interspersed with sniffs and gulps. Bran peered through the overgrown foliage. A dishevelled man with a small owl on his shoulder bowed over a skeletal orang-utan. The man looked up, his tearful eyes searching for signs in the visitor.

Bran smiled. "Ermo? We've come to help."

The keeper looked bewildered. He returned his attentions to the orang-utan, shaking his head. "She's so poorly now, my Gabriela."

He smoothed the wispy aureole of rusty hair around her face. Bran had never seen a primate in such poor condition. The child-like contours of her face had shrunk to saggy chicken flesh and her little eyes would barely open. Her bones looked like they might spear through her thin white skin at the elbows and the hip, and she had lost great patches of hair.

"We can try to help her."

Bran unzipped his backpack of veterinary supplies. The keeper rocked Gabriela, oblivious. Above the sound of Ermo's voice and the tearing of the sterile packaging came sounds of shouting and scuffling and heavy boots on the boardwalk. Bran put down his gear and ran towards the commotion. On the far side of the paved plaza, the soldiers were gathering. A munitions dump had been discovered — the perimeter wall here was close to the quarter of the city where Black Command was based. Shell cases and used rocket parts were piled up with rubble and crude homemade devices in bottles and old drinks cans. Among this detritus were live shells, fat as ripening gourds fit to burst with their deadly seed. The explosives experts set to work on these and everyone else dispersed to safety in the far corners of the Zoo Park. The Mute trailed behind Maria Pequena like a shadow, his fists clenched in excitement, flashing a grin at Bran as he passed.

Rehydration salts were about all Bran had to help Gabriela. Gentle treatment was essential with starvation victims. The keeper was reluctant at first to let him touch her. His face, dark with stubble and worry, kept its hunted look. The little owl opened its beak in threat, running around the keeper's neck to the other shoulder as Bran leant closer to the orang-utan.

"How many animals do you think are still alive?"

Ermo appeared not to hear, smoothing the back of Gabriela's hand.

"We can get them out today. There is a. ceasefire 'til dark."

"Poor Gabriela." Ermo shook his head. The owl preened viciously.

"We brought some food, trucks, but if we don't..."

"Seventy-five." Ermo looked at Bran directly for the first time. "Lonely Orfeo succumbed yesterday, that leaves seventy-five."

Ermo came with Bran to the forecourt, Gabriela cradled in his arms. A sudden booming shook through them and Ermo ducked, bending his body over the orang-utan protectively. The owl fluttered a couple of feet off his shoulder and settled again, squawking in consternation.

"Oh God." Ermo closed his eyes. "They never stop."

"It's okay," Bran said straining to see back into the Park. "I think it's our guys clearing out old shells. Making it safe."

Ermo didn't seem to hear. "You brought these?" He was looking at the vehicles.

"Yes. Can you organise them — sort out which animals can go in each vehicle, so they don't fight or crush each other, more or less?"

A stocky soldier came out from the demolition work, his face smudged with dust.

"All clear now."

Bran left Ermo with the trucks. "We'll need your help later to bring the animals out."

Ermo nodded.

Bran took a bag of grain and went back inside the Park.

Ramiros' fighters patrolled the grounds, locating the live animals and those in most urgent need of attention. Three soldiers found Pata Larga in his small compound of rocks and pollarded trees. They circled the rocky barrier in trepidation at first trying to find access via the keeper's feeding hatch, afraid of a hungry bear's temper. But the once formidable beast, favourite of Ramiros' daughter, was so enfeebled, they realised he'd no strength to strike at them. They clambered into the bear pit with its dried up pond and rotting fish stench. Pata Larga, skinny as a rug, didn't move as they approached, his coat matted and his rump claggy with shit. When they got close, the bear lifted an eyelid. The men halted, afraid that now he might summon his last strength and rise up to strike at them. But the eyelid closed again and the men approached to crouch by him and offer water. They would be able to rope his famous big paws together and make a kind of muzzle after the bear had drunk.

Things were beginning to come together, the passengers roped and ready, but time was short, light sliding from the sky. Bran made his rounds, finding the few still sound cages that would serve during transport. He administered the odd antibiotic injection and cleaned wounds with iodine. He was getting close to counting off Ermo's seventy-five survivors. Calling a nearby soldier he sent him to tie ropes in the open-topped trucks for securing the taller beasts. But the soldier folded his arms in silence and turned away. A second request made no impression. Bran returned to the main plaza and found the other soldiers had downed tools, remonstrating in an angry huddle, punching fists in the air, stabbing pointed fingers towards random corners of the zoo. An eleventh hour mutiny was not what he needed. The voices fell quiet when they noticed Bran approaching. No one would say what the problem was. Bran went back to leading out the first animals along the crooked weed-choked paths, around the uprooted turnstiles to the plaza, a timid tapir and hobbling anteaters.

By the vehicles, Ermo said he'd heard some of the men muttering about stealing animals.

"They say the zoo will be taken beast by beast across the border and given away to the Gauchos, just like always. Is this true?" The keeper spread straw in the back of a jeep. "But I don't care. Take us to the moon, anywhere is better than this hell."

Bran returned to where the soldiers sat, sullen, smoking, amid the carnage and decay. The Mute lingered by the aviary, looking in at the sickly birds with pain in his eyes.

Maria Pequena stepped forwards. "The men want to know what you plan to do with these animals."

"We'll take them to the countryside — to safety, of course."

"But where?"

She cut through the air with opened palms. Behind her soldiers crossed their arms over their chests. "You can't just set a bear loose in Main Street, Aparecido."

"I have friends who run a place in the savannah, they take in rescued animals."

Maria turned to check that the company was following. One soldier, limpet-faced, muttered bitterly. Maria translated, editing the worst offence in the process.

"These, your friends, are they Black Command?"

"No."

"Or Gauchos?"

"No, no, *meu Deus*! They were born right here in this city. Oswaldo did his national service with your Ramiros."

At that the men murmured among themselves and stamped out cigarettes in the dust.

The sky was a glowering pewter stack as they rolled into Santuário das Araras in the wide, swaying *cerrado*. The grassland was a restless sea, the convoy an ark of sorts. The bleached stems closed up behind them, engulfing the trucks and spitting them out like flotsam. Magyar dos Angelos was busy assessing the new arrivals, her brow a serious line as she saw the impact of the war in the far-off city on these creatures. By and by she had them accommodated in a field or an enclosure to suit, and all the beasts had some kind of company, if not of their own kind, then some sympathetic stablemate. Emu with llama, anteater with macaw: nothing that would be prey or predator. Poor Gabriela, thin as a ghost, had no primate companion, not even a spidery little tamarind. But she had her Ermo, and he didn't look like he planned on leaving. Bran stood by the fence looking out over the paddocks to the eternal savannah behind. The soldiers' rough camaraderie, joking and shouting, carried above the noise of the waving grass. Maria Pequena sat on the boot of a jeep with the Mute, silhouetted against the shimmering haematite sky. And Bran, alone by the edge, felt the space of the restless prairie all around him and shivered.

Magyar came over. "We have the otter in a plastic basin for now. Oswaldo will check her paw in the morning. The others'll recover, I think they will. A little time, a lot of food..." She smiled and the fading metallic light gilded her cheek.

Homewards, the convoy set out through the sea of blonde waving stems. Bran found Ermo with Gabriela and gave a squeeze on his shoulder. He jumped behind the wheel and joined the back of the convoy, wondering where he was going home to. Magyar waved them off and went indoors to her Oswaldo. Their house, though just a dot in the desolation of *cerrado*, looked cosy in the mirror.

The *cerrado* was a bowl of emptiness. Bran felt a piece of it, lodged in his gut, a vacuum, a hollowing hunger, settling like a cold stone reaching lake-bottom mud. He drove on across the dancing hay, the gathering darkness on all sides. Behind him, skinny animals settled down in warm nests of straw. And if the storm broke over the Santuário, they would be safe in their pens.

THE DARLING OF BRAZIL

"Dear Kramer,

They say Rio is becoming very dangerous. I worry for you — don't you think of returning to Europe? Here the summer was mild. The almond harvest suffered, according to Senhor Bento. My neighbour Dona Dorothea is very kind, bringing me eggs from her quails. Say hello to The Christ and Ipanema for me. Keep safe. Beijos, Leila."

I miss her. She made everything more beautiful. Now she sends me wistful postcards from Lisbon, while I'm stuck here covering little stories of hatred as the city descends into a drug war that just gets uglier.

As a rookie reporter back then I was unaware of the phenomenon of Leila, until my editor sent me to do a feature on her a few months after getting here. When he warned me not to fall for her, I laughed. I wasn't too crazy about the assignment — research turned up so much sentimental dross about the woman, the kind of hyperbole Brazilians heap on their World Cup heroes. I expected lots of schmaltzy talk too bland to commit to paper. But, not for the first time, Leila defied expectations. For four hours I sat captivated at the Copacabana Palace Hotel. Conversation flowed like we were old childhood buddies. Waiters waltzed around us with endless trays of Brahma beer as I soaked up Leila Camargo's stories of Carnavals past, romances and people she'd met along the way. My tape ran out and I stopped taking notes eventually. The feature wrote itself.

She called to thank me the day after publication. Leila took me under her wing, concerned for a gringo alone in Rio. She pointed out neighbourhoods to avoid, nudged interesting people in my direction, and recommended the city's hidden gems. The biography idea came one morning as I drank my bitter *cafezinho*. It seemed a natural progression from the article. I got sort of obsessed with it and Leila liked the idea, trusted my writing, I guess. A couple of meetings with her agent thrashed out the contract details, and we were ready to go.

She let me shadow her work. Acting assignments and sweaty Carnaval rehearsals, meetings in her favourite haunts, restaurants, beach bars, parks, all the time putting her life onto paper.

That last year in Rio, '94, she was incandescent. It was kind of freakish, not quite normal, for a woman of her years to remain so glamorous. That's one of the great things about Leila, she made her own rules. While her contemporaries retired quietly to their knitting needles, she stuck to what she loved — strutting confidently into the small hours next to silicone-enhanced girls of twenty in samba school rehearsal halls. There was a hiatus when she forsook the parade to pursue novela-acting and charity assignments, but every March she felt a tearing ache when the drums beat in the Sambódromo. When she could bear it no more her old samba school welcomed her back with open arms and the Master of the Bateria chuckled smugly that the rival schools were beaten even before rehearsals began. Since her comeback to the Carnaval scene as a 'dowager' (her word, not mine) in her sixties, she grabbed headlines as much as ever. Her sashaying grew more risqué and stunning each year at the head of the Humming

Bird School drumming corps. Maybe the flesh didn't jiggle so well to the Sambista's rhythms as it once had, but her love of the music never diminished and her lean dancer's legs still caused a furore.

Carnaval 1994 saw Humming Bird's second consecutive win. Leila's familiar, radiant presence, her honed samba paces and the sustained precision of the drumming wowed the judges. The School's motor-floats too were spectacular. 'Community Spirit', that year's theme, was interpreted in entire fibreglass hill-slums complete with kites and goats that teetered on decrepit trucks, inching through the Sambódromo. Leila shimmied, pink tail feathers quivering, like a regal flamingo picking through salt flats. TV screens beamed her megawatt smile into millions of bars and homes. The next day's newspapers gorged on her floodlit features. Her face topped every stack on news-stands from Amazonas to the Pantanal. These were the moments for which Brazil adored her.

Hours after that '94 victory, Leila was special guest on the 'Alô Brasil!' show. Host Vera Veloso spoke rapturously of Leila's Carnaval triumph. Her co-host, 'Captain', a larger-than-life felt parrot, perching on the back of the sofa, flapped his wings in agreement. Vera asked to what her guest attributed her youthful looks. Vera's own bottle-blond beehive and studio-weight make-up looked tired alongside Leila's rosewood complexion.

"Be in love," said Leila. Captain shuffled over and nestled into her neck, crooning. "And if you can't be in love with somebody, fall in love with life itself."

She probably wasn't inventing that for the cameras. Next to beauty and Carnaval, Leila Camargo was famous for love. Romance was almost her calling. She'd been connected with top executives at Petrobras and Brahma Beer, with famous musicians — as Vera now mentioned — and cabinet ministers. She had a son with the Sambista João Ferré and endured a brief marriage to Wanderley das Vigas Barros, the architect fêted for some of Rio's more outré public buildings. She looked like a person sustained by love, velvety mulatto skin that invited touch, full lips stained with Marmara's 'Dark Fig Wine', and sparkling, near-black eyes.

Now she told Vera Veloso, "My other tip is to smile. We Brazilians are joyful people, it doesn't cost a *centavo* to show it, and we're all beautiful with a smile."

Words like these made her a beloved national institution. So much more than Queen of the drumming corps, Leila was a symbol of enduring sensuality, ambassador for Brazil's beauty, warmth and passion, and testimony that even slum girls could hit the Big Time. Increasingly, too, she was hope for women of a certain age that glamour and good looks need not be the exclusive preserve of the young.

The press clippings I'd unearthed, showed how Leila's beauty combined with a natural ambassadorial quality had made her a very bankable commodity, appealing right across the social spectrum. Her interviews could be the words of any housewife, she was so quotably ordinary.

"In the morning I have papaya slices with Mineiro cheese and a good strong cup of 'Pestle' coffee." (Pestle was the brand she endorsed for a half million *reais* a year).

Her patriotic diet of grocery store staples was within reach, gave people hope. The Carnaval Darling's escape from dire poverty was legendary, yet she still ate the same daily bread as most Brazilians.

"It's a career to be proud of, darling," said Vera. "All Brazil is proud. You're truly loved."

They kissed goodbye, and Leila waved to the audience.

"Go with God, *querida*," said Vera, kissing her fingers and dusting them towards her retreating guest. Captain feigned a swoon.

We watched the clip of her TV interview at Leila's holiday place in Búzios, the beach resort made famous by Brigitte Bardot. The cook had brewed coffee, its rich scent mingling with the ocean air. I waited in the hall while on the terrace the maid rinsed linens, singing 'Disillusion' in a doleful voice. Normally she sang 'Soap It Up, Mulatta' or some other brisk working song to get through the laundering hours. Something about the change of tune and that maudlin voice bothered me, though I couldn't work out why.

Finally Leila emerged and we installed ourselves on the front veranda where ferns hanging in baskets cast ragged shade. She set her little green coffee cup on the tiles beside her feet, disturbing a gecko that scuttled under the steps.

"So I've been working on the material about Carnaval costumes over the decades. You were quite the trailblazer." We had looked through Leila's albums, complete archives of Carnaval's bold fashions. From early sepia images, with mid-calf hemlines and demure cloche-hats through fifties dirndls that lifted as dancers spun, revealing a little leg, to the recent images where costumes involved so much fabric — feathers, tulle, sequins — yet so very little coverage.

Leila laughed. "In the sixties bikinis and spangled shorts were the thing. I loved the freedom of movement. Raimundo Carnavalesco, the all-powerful parade designer, was already pushing for tinier costumes. He replaced

172

shorts with string bikinis under voile tunics in '69, I think. Each year he'd stand over the seamstresses shouting 'Cut, *querida*, more,' until only tiny scraps of fabric remained. They barely stayed in place. Then, he axed the tunics. Just bikinis. Ee! I had to drink a little *aguardente* first."

Famously, Leila had stood under the Sambódromo's galaxy of lights, wearing only swirls of paint in Humming Bird's signature pink and white. Sequins over her nipples and strips of flesh-coloured theatrical tape, tactically positioned, kept her on the right side of the 'no nudity' rule. After Leila, other Samba schools' queens dared to parade wearing only paint.

"At first I felt vulnerable, I moved differently. But actually, you feel less exposed in paint than those tiny bikinis. And ah, *meu Deus*, they make a masterpiece of you."

"You came full circle from the days when your only clothes were cousins' hand-me-downs," I smiled, scribbling 'feel less exposed' in my notebook.

No one knew much about Leila's life before she was famous, just that it was dirt poor. For me, she recalled in detail the two-room shack where her mother raised her and her brothers. She and her mother left to clean for the Mayor's wife each day at dawn. She remembered the grim state of *Mamãe* at nights, half-collapsing after hours of scrubbing, and the mayoress's venomous comments. Leila would never forget the mudslide that nearly swept them all away as they slept, nor the worry of her brothers' regular fevers.

Most clearly of all she recalled the day Mayor Waldez caught her dancing with a broom on the veranda, how her cheeks burnt like brazier coals as the tall man made to speak but instead left in silence, an unfathomable look on his face. For three long days her stomach churned, waiting for dismissal — and the shame that went with it — and the end of life as they knew it. She was shaking, speechless when the Mayor came looking for her with, instead of angry words, a dress — beaded wine taffeta — and an announcement. She was to ride in the Carnaval parade in front of all Rio, and dance Samba.

So, at eighteen the apprentice maid given to waltzing with brooms sambaed into the mayor's retinue among a cavalcade of glossy open-top Buicks. Riding alongside were the coffee barons of Petrópolis, the governor and his cronies, and theatrical stars from the Chiquinha Gonzaga Company. The girls wore long frocks, dolly-shoes and stockings that were a torment in the February heat. The surf was high on Copacabana and the crowds lining Avenida Atlantica waved their handkerchiefs and cheered.

I was lost for a moment in these borrowed memories, a lullaby of distant samba and waves flopping on the shore. Leila owed this luxurious beachfront view to the long-ago whim of Rio's Mayor who turned his maid into a Carnaval debutante.

"How did your husband react to your minimal costumes and all the media attention in the seventies?" I wondered, imagining if it were me, that I'd not be the understanding liberal she might have hoped for. She had been so open with me about her past relationships — many had been chronicled in the newspapers anyway — I felt comfortable asking. She never mentioned anyone current, though I had a feeling there was someone.

She sighed. "Wanderley and I had split by then. But there was someone — let's say a very influential man. He wasn't jealous at all. Always said he was the luckiest man in Brazil."

On the evening bus back to Rio, I mused on life's lottery, how destiny could pick out a girl resigned to sweeping floors for important men, and turn her into a sequinned celebrity. That day in Paraíso, the favela where Leila grew up, two girls had been shot. They were walking to their cleaning jobs, innocents caught in crossfire over drug territory. The bus nosed into the suburbs. Across the aisle, stark headlines on a discarded newspaper declared civil war in the favelas. The police spokesmen stuck to their lines, without apparent irony, about cleaning up the slums and making them safe. Favela residents told a different story: the drug lords at least kept order in neighbourhoods where police were never seen. Among all the bold font sound bites and hyperbolic headlines, it was hard to find real figures for the death toll, or any facts about the victims, or who'd been shot by who.

Days later, Leila called to say our reminiscing had put her in a nostalgic mood and she wanted to indulge it. The place to pursue such a moment was Café Colombo in central Rio. Leila was taken there after her first Carnaval. I'd made notes on the place for the book — a famous old Viennese coffee house lined with ornate, freckled mirrors — and was keen to see it for real. Just as I was leaving, Leila rang again.

"Darling, it's chaos here. The maid disappeared yesterday; went out for eggs and Chlorox and hasn't been back. Can we make it four instead?"

I set off anyway, planning to soak up the atmosphere until she arrived. Thick glass oblongs in the café's swing doors framed a sedate afternoon crowd demanding little of the staff. I pressed on the brass fingerplates; the scent of coffee and caramelised sugar enveloped me. Doodling on a napkin, among crystal cake stands and copper urns, I pictured young, timid Leila, swept along by the Governor's entourage, trying not to stare. In my mind, waiters in white arranging fancy china made her blush and she was silent, afraid her untutored voice would remind someone she belonged in domestic service instead of the mayoral cavalcade.

And then there she was in the doorway, confident, no trace of timidity now. I waved. As she moved towards me she looked, smiling, towards the bar, seeking familiar faces. The headwaiter hadn't seen her, his face, serious, cast down apparently busy with paper work.

"Mm...doesn't it smell good?" We kissed cheeks and sat, breathing in caramel and coffee-scented nostalgia. "Sorry to keep you. Have you chosen? I'm going for my usual — Belém custard pie." She winked conspiratorially.

"I'll go with that. Any news of the maid?"

"No. I don't know what to think."

"Did you call the police?"

"Not yet — I kept hoping she would just come back. *Meu Deus*, what a mess." She looked expectantly towards the bar. "Usually they're more attentive. The Paraguayan guy always has a funny story, let's catch his eye."

But the Paraguayan waiter looked with fierce concentration at glasses he was polishing. She beckoned, fig-painted nails lustrous in the café's amber lighting. He turned, lifting a tray to embark on a glass-collecting circuit. Normally in public places, Leila was welcomed with smiles and kisses, not indifference. Reasserting her poise she waved forcefully, this time towards the headwaiter, too close to ignore her. He approached, eyes towards the floor, something carried behind his back.

"*Querido* — are you going to let us die of thirst today?"

Her eyes creased and her lips spread into an irresistible fig-wine smile. But the waiter returned a marble face. It was hard to say what sentiment his stony features were transmitting, except that it was bad.

"Heraldo, for the love of God, what happened?" Leila inclined her face towards him.

The waiter's arms unclasped from behind his back, swishing that morning's *Jornal do Brasil* through the air and onto our table. He straightened it for her to read. All around, customers looked up from their pies and cream coffees, stealing furtive glances in the grand mirrors. The headline ran, 'O Diamante Escandaloso.' Leila, shaking her head slowly, seemed to be struggling to read. I, being a hack, could read newsprint upside down and back to front.

"Carnaval Queen Camargo... hoarded a diamond pendant... undisclosed value... inscribed 'All my love, Emílio'... sources close to the celebrated dancer revealed..." A small picture of her punctuated the first column, the word 'Shamed' below. A shot of a diamond necklace dominated the remaining text.

Her almost-black eyes squinted.

"Confirming..." the column went on, "a secret affair..." in bold, and finally, "with hated Dictator, Emílio Garrastazú Médici..." The last column concluded, "...an infamous regime of torture and murders."

Leila's eyes returned to Heraldo's accusing glare. She rose unsteadily and fled the café's mirrored cocoon.

I ran after her. She rounded the corner of a parking lot, gasping. Her driver sat in the attendant's cabin craning his neck like a goose towards a tiny TV on a high shelf showing the Flu-Fla game. By his wary look, it seemed he too had been tainted by the news. Nonetheless he fetched the car. Jobs like his were not thrown away lightly.

"Please, Kramer." She put a hand over mine on her forearm. "You should go now."

I protested.

She pushed me gently, "Go."

She turned away, her heeled sandals fidgeting in the dust.

"Emílio," she said quietly. "I knew him as 'Emilinho' or 'Mimí'. No 'Médici'. Never 'Dictator'."

I nodded.

I took a cab. The traffic moved like cold treacle, gumming up the tunnels that bore through Rio's hills. On the corner of Jardim Botânico, idle taxi drivers read newspapers with the engraved locket on the front. I imagined Leila in her car crawling towards Ipanema, realising that the story of her affair with Médici, reviled dictator of the military years, meant that from this day, she was Brazil's darling no more. Rio was no longer her city. Leaning my head against the window, I wondered how much she could allow herself to connect the maid's disappearance with the story of her locket on the front pages. I remembered her words, "She went out for eggs... I just kept hoping she'd come back." After years of adulation, perhaps it wasn't easy to believe in betrayal and ill will. Just days ago, crowds in the Sambódromo had roared for her. Now she'd have to pack up and leave by the back door. I knew then the biography was over too.

She fled to Europe.

For several months I left it alone. While gangs and police carved up the slums I wrote turgid little stories for the magazine. I missed Leila — like I said, she made everything more beautiful, more fun. Somehow she distracted people from grievances and violence. She seemed to inhabit another sphere, a light-filled world free from weapons and drugs, poverty and mudslides. And yet, as everyone knew, she was a child of those destitute slum lands herself.

Then, quite abruptly, I decided to track down the maid. Curiosity I guess, about why she did it and whether, living among all the violence, her life was any better now. Riane Barcellos had gone to live with family in Roçinha, Rio's largest favela. The house was having proper plastering over its bare brick façade, perhaps thanks to the newspaper fee. Riane was watering mint planted in old oilcans. She didn't want to talk.

When I turned to go, finally she spoke, as if this were the only chance to air her defence.

"Thirty years I worked for her." She swung the dregs from the watering can. "Médici put my cousin in jail you know, for organising sugarcane workers. Beat him up good, too. We never saw him again. Meanwhile, Dona Leila's drinking wine with that criminal, making like he's Clark Gable. And there's me washing up the wineglasses like a fool."

And she turned to go in doors again.

But I couldn't leave. "It doesn't make sense — your cousin, that was in the military years. Why wait 'til now?"

She didn't want to talk any more. She went indoors and I was left, bewildered, frustrated beside a half-finished wall that bounded the property, misshapen iron pins worming from the last row of bricks. The noise of the favela — backfiring engines, barking dogs, Pagode music and people shouting over back fences — reminded me I was a stranger here, an eavesdropper on other people's conversations, other people's lives. I turned to go back down the hill.

"Sir." Riane was at the door again. "This was why."

I walked back, climbed over the wall. She showed me a newspaper cutting unfolded from an envelope. It was about the police 'clean up' operation in two of Rio's biggest slums, begun some months earlier. The official targets were the leaders of drug cartels that controlled these neighbourhoods. The actual victims, as ever, were ordinary residents.

Riane had let her resentment stew gently over the decades, reducing, becoming a dark viscose syrup, bitter, deep in her marrow, dense pools collected in the bends of her viscera. Perhaps it would have simmered away to nothing — a burnt residue, the sort that can be scraped from the bottom of a bean pan with a spoon — if nothing had been added to reconstitute it.

I stared hard at the fragile cutting. She looked at me with a faint disappointment. She flipped the cutting fully open. There was a photo of the Chief of Police on the other side of the fold. Leila, with her fatal sense of timing, had been dating him around the time of the attack on the slums. That was the spark that re-ignited the flame under the pot, setting Riane's anger on the boil again, like cane brandy sousing an over-thickened sauce, loosening, making it soupy, thin enough to pour into long-empty spaces. Hot. Reviving.

I think Leila really didn't read the news. If she did, she couldn't link it to her life, to romance. Love was excusable, immune, in a higher category. She was the kind of person who would never ask what you did for a living, but instead about what was your passion, what was the music you loved most, your memories of a certain place, which foods always brought back good feelings. What did you think of the music of Chiquinha Gonzago and wasn't it time her songs were re-recorded?

Leila's eventual letter, sending an address in Lisbon, came as a relief. Her words were kind, polite, but without the easy openness we'd shared before, revealing nothing about her feelings. No doubt she thought about Riane's betrayal — who else had access to her jewellery boxes — but we never mentioned it.

For the crime of loving the wrong person, a nation turned its back on Leila. Feminists despised her because they said that for Médici, women did not exist. She would never understand that. He'd treated her like a goddess. Environmentalists hated her for loving a man to whom forests were land to be cleared for cash crops. Yet she described to me a man so moved by the beauty of an orchid he brought her that his eyes filled with tears. (It bloomed defiantly in her apartment for years after the affair was over). To the many whose relatives disappeared or suffered at the hands of Médici henchmen, she was a traitor. Leila understood only that the people she loved had turned against her, and she must live apart from her beloved Brazil. She had no notion of the many species of hatred people nurtured for her. When she told me of the affair, she had kept the dictator's identity secret. Not, I think, from any sense of shame or self-preservation, but to protect him. His gestures and gifts, despite their destructive impact on her life, remained unsullied, being given in love. Leila seemed naively detached from the brutal politics of the man. She was able to love his present tense, a gentle lover pouring wine, tracing her collarbone, and preserve that facet of him, that sliver of kindness, like an insect wing in amber, never wondering how he filled the hours they spent apart.

I had chosen a postcard of Christ the Redeemer for my wistful Leila in Lisbon. The nib of my pen hesitated over the blank space. Where to start? She'd heard of the ugly violence and soaring death rates in her Rio. How should I explain the rumours to one so famous for love and beauty? Should I offer cheap philosophy, saying anyone can grow bitter, tempted to sell secrets, if life treats them harshly like Riane Barcellos?

"Leila, Querida, ..." I began. *"The Ipê trees are blossoming like crazy this year along Nossa Senhora de Copacabana. It must be all that rain we had. Wish you could be here to see it."*